MOTHER
CONDEMNED

Published by Lulu

Copyright © 2015 by
Jodi Clark All Rights
Reserved

ISBN #978-0-9891207-6-0

Printed in the United States of America

MOTHER CONDEMNED

By Jodi Clark

Chapter 1

Crash! Shattering glass pierced the tranquil night, violently jolting Lauri awake. She sprung up in bed, paralyzed with fear and her heart pounding against her chest as the rustling of an intruder echoed through the house and the possibility for anything existed. Panic overcame her while she reached for the knife that she kept in the drawer of her nightstand. As a single mother, she was left to defend her household alone, and it terrified her.

She was desperate to get to her five year old son, who was asleep in his bedroom down the hall of the undersized rancher. Her entire body quaked with terror as she scanned her bedroom for anything else that could be used as a weapon while she frantically dialed 911. "Someone is in my house!" She whispered to the dispatcher in a panic. "Someone broke in. I need help!"

"The intruder is in your house right now?" The calm voice clarified.

"Yes, I'm in my bedroom and I can hear rustling, I think in the living room," the horrified woman exclaimed.

"Please, hurry." Her heart pounded so hard that she swore it would explode.

"Okay, stay on the line with me," the dispatcher commanded calmly. "I have police officers in route."

"I have to get my son." The voice on the phone advised against Lauri leaving her bedroom, but she put the phone down and grabbed the heavy porcelain lamp from her nightstand. She had always been against guns and refused to have one in the house, especially with a young child there but, at that moment, she wished that she had one and hoped that whoever it was in her house didn't. Quietly, she made her way toward the door in the darkened room, determined to get to Benny. The rustling had suddenly ceased, leaving only the tremble of her breath, and she wondered what the intruder was doing as she prepared to face him. Lauri had no idea how many invaders were in her house or what they wanted. They could have been there to rob her, rape her or even kill her, she thought, and the worst of many different scenarios sped through her mind. She wondered if the intruder had heard her on the phone. The silence only intensified her fear as she imagined the stranger sneaking up on her the way that she stalked him. She slowly approached her bedroom door, peeking out into the hallway, lit only by a nightlight. Her heart sped as she tiptoed down the hallway toward Benny's room as quietly and quickly as she could, praying that the old, wooden floor didn't do its usual creaking. The faint sound of sirens lent confidence. The careful trek to her son's bedroom felt like it took forever as she cautiously made her way there with the knife trembling in her unsteady hand, fully prepared to use it if she needed to. Lauri finally reached his bedroom to find his bed empty with the blankets pulled down. She could hardly see anything in the dark but managed to shut and lock his bedroom door.

"Benny," she whispered, thinking that he had heard the burglar and was hiding. She opened his closet door and looked under his bed but still saw no sign of him. She scurried to turn on the light switch and found his room vacant. Lauri scurried to the bathroom in search of him but found it empty, as well. "Benny!" She yelled for her son in frantic desperation for him, no longer even aware of the possible dangers. "Don't panic," she told herself. Her fear was suddenly replaced by the need to find him as she began searching the house. Frantically, she opened cabinets and checked in closets, even running outside and into the garage. "Benny!" She screamed out desperately. "Benny!" She screamed, over and over, running through the house. "Benny!" There was no answer. The intruder was gone and with him, her only child.

Four police officers parked in front of her house, their blue lights laminating the other houses and waking the neighbors. Three stood behind their cars on the barren street, with guns drawn, while another cautiously approached the front door and slowly opened it to find her in hysterics.

"Ma'am, are you okay?" He asked with urgency in his voice. "Is the intruder still in the house?"

"My son!" She spouted with panic. He was her only concern and that was all that she could utter at that moment.

"Ma'am, is there anyone else in the house?" The officer repeated in an escalating tone as the others began searching rooms. "Your son is in the house?"

"He took him!" Laurie screamed, helplessly dropping to her knees. "Benny's gone! Please, we have to find him, now!"

"Ma'am, calm down," the officer replied, as if she really could. "Did you see the intruder?" He calmly queried.

"No, I was in my bedroom, on the phone with 911," she answered with drenched eyes. "Oh, God, please find my baby!" She felt like she was suffocating, not knowing where her son was or what was happening to him. She imagined him terrified and crying for her, and she couldn't stand the thought of it as she struggled to catch her breath.

"Do you know how the intruder might have gotten inside the house? Were the doors and windows locked?"

"I think he broke a window," she answered. "I heard glass breaking. That's what woke me up."

The police officer peered at his partner, who was glancing back, skeptical of the woman's story. The two officers continued their interview with her, and her agitation cultivated until she finally exploded.

"Stop questioning me and find my son!" She demanded with agony, and two police officers left the house to scour the area. She was hysterical with the worst-case scenarios plaguing her mind and, the longer the police waited, the further away her son was likely going, she thought.

"Ma'am, you have to calm down," the officer scolded. "We can't find your son without your cooperation." Lauri complied, struggling to pull herself together, and sat down on the couch to answer the officers' questions while they awaited investigators to evaluate the scene. "Okay, now explain to me exactly what happened," the officer commanded as he took out his notepad and pen. He took notes as she described the breaking glass in the rear of the house that woke her, the 911 call, the rustling noises in her house and, finally, discovering her son missing. She couldn't believe what had occurred, and she was overcome with helplessness as she struggled to maintain her composure. All she wanted to do was look for her son, and it aggravated her that the officers seemed more concerned with the trespasser than her missing child.

"Did you get any description at all of the intruder or hear any voices?" The officer asked. "Was there more than one person? Was the intruder was male or female?" The unending questions continued.

"I told you, I was in my bedroom, on the phone

with 911," Lauri repeated. "All I heard was rustling, no voices, but it sounded like possibly just one person. I never saw anyone. I only heard him."

"Uh huh, and did you happen to see a vehicle outside?"

"No!" she snapped, frustrated with all of the questions. She felt that the officers were wasting precious time. The more time they spent with her, the further away the kidnapper was getting with her child. "Please, I've told you every single thing I know."

Two investigators arrived and began looking around Laurie's house for clues, finding a window near the back door shattered. They dusted the broken window for fingerprints before checking Benny's bedroom for clues.

"The glass is broken from the outside," one noted. They scoured the house and searched outside for footprints or tire tracks.

"Anything?" One officer asked the investigators while the other continued his conversation with Lauri.

"Just a broken window so far," the middle- aged, gray-haired detective replied, lighting a cigarette. "She didn't see anything at all? No glimpse of the suspect?"

"Nothing." He sighed, "Says she was on the line with 911 in her bedroom." His tone was lackluster and suspicious.

"We need the tape," the investigator said, and with that, he approached the horrified mother. "Ms. Felder, I'm Detective Nelson. I realize what a difficult time this is for you, but we're going to need you to go down to the station for a few more questions." She angrily sprung up from the couch.

"Listen, I've been answering your questions for the last hour," she huffed with her finger in his face, like a woman who had gone mad. "I've told you everything I know and now, I just want to find my son!" She grabbed a recent photo of Benny in a wooden frame from a nearby stand and gave it to the detective. "Help me find him." With her head in her hands, she fell back to the couch, wailing over her missing child. She was living her worst nightmare. The investigator assured her that they would do everything they could but he insisted on driving her to the police station.

"It's just protocol that we have to follow," he assured her. "Please try and understand that. We have to check out everyone." The drive to the station seemed endless as Lauri stared out the window, wondering where Benny could be.

"How did this happen?" She thought, pinching her arm in hopes of the whole thing being simply a horrible nightmare that she would wake herself from as she pleaded with God for Benny's return.

"Ma'am, I want you to know that we have a lot of good officers out looking for your son," the driver assured her. "I can promise you that they are doing everything in their power to locate him." His words didn't lend her much comfort, but nothing could at that time. All she wanted was to hold her child and know that he was safe.

When they reached their destination, the questioning reconvened in a drab and undersized interrogation room, and she felt like a criminal sitting in the metal chair.

"Would you like some coffee or water?" Detective Nelson inquired and she shook her head. "Ms. Felder, how is your relationship with your son?" He asked her while lighting a cigarette. The smell nauseated her, and she found herself extremely annoyed that he hadn't respected her by asking first. The other part of her wanted to have one with him to calm her nerves.

"We have a great relationship," she sobbed. "He's my baby boy and I love him more than life." The tears reconvened in her grieving eyes and the detective handed her a tissue.

"What about his father? Is he in the picture?" Laurie sighed, almost ashamed at her answer.

"His father is in prison and has been for a while," she began. "Drugs got the best of him and, because of that, he's only been around at his convenience. Now, of course, he's not around at all." She still harbored a lot of anger toward her ex-husband for allowing drugs to destroy their family and leaving her to pick up the pieces.

"Is there any communication between him and the child?"

"Not since his rights were taken away, which has been a few years ago." She recalled the tough road that she and Benny had travelled together without his father around, both financially and emotionally. She had been forced to get a second job, just to make ends meet, and that was hardly enough. Moreover and even worse to her was having to console their son and make excuses for his father not being present. She certainly wasn't willing to take him for prison visitations, but she didn't want Benny to think less of him amid their divorce, in spite of how she felt. Benny, especially, had had a difficult time adjusting. He was too young to understand the true impact of drug abuse. Lauri had been raising her son by herself since he was two years old and, though it wasn't always easy, it was always worth it because he was the best thing that had ever happened to her. He was her everything.

The investigators asked the same questions, over and over again.

"Do you struggle financially, Ms. Felder?"

"Of course I do. I'm a single mother."

"Do you know of anyone who would want to harm you or your son?" The detective probed.

"No."

"Have you ever tried to harm yourself or your child?"

"Of course not!" She blurted. "What kind of

question is that?"

"Ms. Felder, do you have a life insurance policy on your son?" The investigator had gone too far, she thought. The longer they probed, the more critical of her they appeared to grow. It was as if they felt she had planned the whole thing. "Forgive me, but I'm struggling to understand how this happened," the menacing detective said in his gruff tone. "Someone broke into your house and allegedly kidnapped your son, but there was nothing in array or stolen and you didn't see anything. There are no prints and not one thing to go on."

"What are you implying?" Laurie glared at him from across the small table with disdainful eyes, appalled at being treated as a suspect. "Am I being legally detained or may I go now? I need to go find my son!" The detective reluctantly released her but the investigation would continue.

On her way out the door, he interjected, "We would like to put a tap on your phone, just in case the kidnapper should call." Laurie readily agreed, hoping for any indication of where Benny was. She was thankful to have recently taught her son their telephone number. "An Amber Alert will soon be put out with the photo you supplied to us, and it would be helpful if you went before the media to plead for your son's return."

"Of course," Lauri complied. It was the first ounce of compassion that he had offered. "I want to do whatever it takes."

That night, after the bustle of the police in and out had ceased for the day, Lauri's house was desolate and quiet, and the silence was overwhelming. Ordinarily, Benny would have been in the living room, watching cartoons or playing a game and she still envisioned him there but, with him gone, the house was nearly unbearable to be in, and she didn't know what to do. Nothing could take her mind off of her child, and she wanted to keep looking for him. She opened the door to his room of light blue walls and his favorite cartoon characters. An array of his toys were still strewn about the floor where he'd been playing with him before going to bed that fateful night. The room still felt like him, smelled like him, and she hoped that it could, somehow, offer her some answers.

"How could this have happened?" She thought as she sat on her son's bed, tearfully yearning for him, desperately missing him. Lauri blamed herself. If only she had gotten to the kidnapper sooner, ran to Benny's room instead of dialing 911 first, everything might be different. She couldn't sleep, her mind refusing to rest from wondering where Benny was and if he was safe, or even still alive. It tortured every part of her to feel so helpless and unable to help him. "Why did they come for him?" She wondered. They hadn't stolen anything or tried to harm her in any way but seemingly just wanted her young son. She needed to know why. That night, in his bed, she took her mind through every single person she knew, every person in her life, both past and present, analyzing each in her mind and asking who would have a motive to take him. She hugged his pillow tightly, smelling him and yearning for him, praying for him, until she cried herself to sleep.

The next morning, under a dismal sky and rain-beaten sidewalks, a search party of concerned family, friends, neighbors and strangers from the community split up into groups to search for the young boy. They knocked on neighborhood doors, scoured the streets, wooded areas, yards and even dumpsters, desperate for a clue to Benny's whereabouts. Lauri prayed that someone would find something that could lead her to her child. She knew that he could have been with anyone, and she feared the abductor's intentions, but she refused to allow herself to think the worst. As long as no one found a body, there was a chance he was still alive, and it was that tiny glimmer of hope that gave her strength. She wanted him to know that they were all looking for him, that no one would give up the search. She wouldn't let them. She prayed that he was safe and that he knew how much she loved him. Reporters from the local and regional newspapers and television stations began to arrive to do live reports on the missing child. Lauri was astonished by the amount of support that she was receiving from the community, many of whom she had never even met. They were all there to help find her son, and it meant everything to her.

"Can you believe this?" Her mother said with her arm around her shoulder and a grateful smile. "They are all here for our little boy."

"I can't thank them all enough. It's incredible." Their compassion brought the all too familiar tears back to Lauri's face. She was thankful for the support, especially amid accusations from the police that she was responsible. Tears streamed down her cheeks as she stood before the television camera, begging for son's kidnapper to release him.

"My son is missing," she began, holding up a photo of him. "Please, if anyone has seen him or knows anything at all, even if you think it's not relevant, please come forward and help me find my baby. You don't have to give your name or any other information. All Benny has is me. He needs his mother," she mournfully pleaded. "I beg whoever took him to let him go, even if it's anonymously."

She wondered where Benny could be and who he was with, and she prayed that he was safe. The thought of him being afraid and crying for her plagued her every single second. She wondered why someone had chosen him. She needed to know that he was being taken care of, and she prayed with all of her soul that he was still alive. It tormented her to think of her child being abused or intimidated. Lauri prayed for her son to be found, safe. Her world had come to a halt and she wasn't able to function without him. She was desperate to hold him in her arms again.

Chapter 2

"Any leads yet?" Detective Nelson asked his partner at the police station as he descended into the black leather chair at his desk while struggling to keep his tie out of his cup of coffee.

"Not much," his lanky partner answered with a sigh. "We've talked to neighbors, relatives, friends, even school officials. One neighbor claims to have heard glass breaking at around 3 a.m., but she didn't see anyone. No one seems to know anything."

With his feet crossed on his desk, sipping his coffee, Detective Nelson brainstormed. "We got the 911 tape but there's nothing out of the ordinary," he said with a deep breath. "A person breaks a window in the middle of the night and steals a child, yet no one saw anything. No one saw the intruder, no one saw a getaway car, nothing." The undersized, plump detective rubbed the stubble on his chin in deep thought. "Where is this kid, John?" He pondered, staring off in thought. "We have no witnesses and no evidence, not even a fingerprint and hell, the house wasn't even ransacked. It's like he disappeared into thin air. Whoever it was that broke into that house wanted that kid and nothing else." The detectives knew that it was a kidnapping rather than a robbery, and they knew how crucial the first forty-eight hours were. The longer Benny was gone, the slimmer the chances were of finding him alive.

"Someone out there knows something," John replied.

"What do we have on the mother?"

"We ran a full check on her, and she's clean other than a couple of parking tickets and some mounting debt. Everyone I talked with insists that she's the average doting mother. She does have a life insurance policy on the boy, taken out last year."

"Really? Hmm," Detective Nelson nodded, "and she's the only one who knows what happened."

"You don't think she did it, do you?" His partner probed.

"I don't know," he answered, "but people who need money are capable of some pretty desperate acts sometimes, so I'm not ruling it out just yet."

Lauri posted photos of Benny everywhere that she could. She covered telephone poles and trees, store windows, bulletin boards and newspapers in hopes that someone would recognize her son. His kidnapper could have taken him out of the state and they could have been anywhere. She thought about all of the times she had seen reports of missing children. Never had she thought hers would become one of them. A few of the lucky ones had been found, and usually not far from their neighborhoods, but most were still missing, and she could never understand where so many missing people could be in the world without being found. It was her worst fear. Her life depended on getting him Benny back. She was afraid that, in time, the police would give up looking for the child, and she refused to let that happen. If it took the rest of her life, she would never stop searching for him.

Her life had come to a complete standstill. She couldn't eat, couldn't sleep, couldn't work and her only goal was to find her missing son. With him gone, she was only a ghost of herself, and she felt like she was drowning. Her heart ached more than she had ever known possible, and her soul screamed out for Benny. On her knees, she prayed.

"God, I know that I haven't done everything right. I know that I haven't always been the person you wanted me to be and that I need a lot of improvement, but my little Benny is innocent, and he needs his mother, so please, God, please bring him back home safely." She knew that he had heard her desperation, and a sense of comfort rushed through her, lending her hope that Benny was alright.

Her mother and friends had been with her throughout the entire ordeal, consoling her and helping her post Benny's photos around town. They had never known such heartache as they felt then, with their friend's son missing and Lauri so distraught, and there was nothing they could do to fix it. It made them weary in their own homes and fearful for their own children because no one knew when the kidnapper would strike again. Mothers were forced to talk to their children about strangers and kidnapping and what to do if a stranger approached them. The children in the community were plagued with questions, and school counselors were on hand to help with them.

Detective Nelson returned to question Lauri again, this time about the life insurance policy on Benny.

"Is there any particular reason that you bought life insurance for your son?" He bluntly probed.

"Why is that so unusual?" She responded defensively. Nearly everyone she knew carried life insurance on their children.

"If you don't mind, Ms. Felder, I'll ask the questions." She rolled her eyes with frustration at his tough talking persona.

"Actually, I do mind, but I bought the policy for him because I believe that everyone should have life insurance. I'm a single mother, Detective and God forbid, if something…." Her statement was interrupted by her tears and her fear of the worst. "If something happened, I would need that insurance to help… to help bury…" Again, she broke down. The detective took a deep breath and allotted her a few minutes to pull herself together but offered no consolation to the grieving mother.

"He's awfully young, just being five years old," the investigator stated. "Does he have a will, too?"

"You bastard!" She roared, leaping up from her

chair. "I don't know what you're implying but Benny also has medical insurance and a savings account," Lauri responded irately. "Would you like to analyze those also?"

Detective Nelson motioned to the cigarette in his hand. "May I?" He inquired.

"No."

"Okay then," he said, calmly placing it back in his shirt pocket. "Why are you so defensive? These are not uncommon questions."

"With all due respect, Detective, I'm defensive because you seem to be accusing me of something instead of doing your damn job!" She seethed. "I think it's time that I retain an attorney. Maybe he can help find my son."

"Do you feel that you need one?" He probed smoothly with the intention of making her crack.

"Yes, I do feel like I need one!" she snipped. "Then he can answer your questions while I look for Benny."

"No one is accusing you, Ms. Felder," he responded. "In fact, I do sympathize with you. I understand the pain you're going through. I'm just doing my job. I have to talk to everyone in a case like this, especially the parents."

"Well, I have been very cooperative and now, we need to be looking for my child," Lauri firmly concluded with a stare. "If you have kids of your own, then you understand that." She closed the door behind her and, once again, broke down. She felt like she was living a nightmare. Benny was gone, maybe even dead, and not knowing his condition tortured her every minute. She couldn't breathe without him, and her life depended on him being found. She knew that she would never be the same without him. She couldn't even imagine living without her son. He was her entire world. In her mind, Lauri analyzed every person that she had ever had contact with for a clue as to who might have taken Benny. Her family was immediately ruled out, Benny's father was in prison and she didn't suspect any of her friends or neighbors. There was not even one person in her life that she felt could have taken her son, nor could she conjure up a reason for his kidnapping. It had to be a stranger that had possibly been watching them, she thought. She was fighting to remain strong in what felt like a hopeless situation. A piece of her died with every minute that he was gone and, if that wasn't enough to bear, Lauri appeared to be under suspicion in Benny's disappearance. Nothing made sense to her. There were no answers. She prayed that it was all just a horrific nightmare that she would soon awaken from. Lauri was grateful that her friends and mother were there to offer support. She desperately needed someone around who was on her side, someone who could aid in the search for Benny rather than focusing on finding someone to blame. Lauri didn't feel that the police were doing an efficient job of looking for Benny and, though they continued to reassure her that their search was vigilant, they appeared to already be treating the case like a murder. Her tears were the only release that she had as she fell to her knees, pleading with God.

"Please, please bring him home, God. Please keep my baby safe," she begged.

At the police station, callers periodically reported potential sightings of Benny, and Detective Nelson and his partner had been investigating each one. Donations from the community were put up as a reward for information leading to the child in hopes that it would bring new information. Each new lead brought hope for Lauri that her son was still alive, but every one seemed to be an unfortunate case of mistaken identity or a quest for the reward.

"I just don't understand how someone could take a child from his mother and his home," Lauri told her friends one evening as they sat in her living room. "Why would they take him?"

"We're going to get him back, honey," her lifelong

friend, Jessica, assured with her arm around her. "We will."

"She's right," Carla, her friend from work, added. "There are a lot of people out there searching for him and praying for his return, and that is so powerful."

"I know that," Lauri replied with swollen, tear-soaked eyes, "and I'm trying so hard to stay positive. I'm just so thankful that you all are here. It really helps me through the days."

"We wouldn't be anywhere else," Carla told her.

"When are your mom and sister flying in?" Jessica asked.

"They're coming in the day after tomorrow. I'm picking them up from the airport at three."

"Do you want me to go with you?" Jessica asked. "I don't mind."

"Thanks but I'll be fine," Lauri insisted. "Besides, I need to get out of this house for a bit."

In the tiny, safe town where everyone seemed to know one another, crimes like burglary and kidnapping didn't occur. Everyone had always felt secure in their homes, and some didn't even lock their doors. Lauri's story had rapidly become the buzz in the small Georgia town, and her home was transformed into a campsite for a frenzy of reporters, brazenly snapping photos through her windows and calling her on the phone. She was suddenly a hostage in her own home with the blinds closed and continuous knocks on the door, pleading for a statement from her. In her sporadic treks from her house, she was fiercely hounded by reporters.

"Are you a suspect in this case?" A reporter asked with a microphone up to her face.

"Do the police have any leads?" Another probed while camera flashes blinded her eyes. Continuous questions from the slew of reporters following her to her car pierced her ears.

"I'm just trying to find my son," was Lauri's only

comment, and she flashed his photo to the camera. "Please, if anyone knows anything at all, come forward. I need him home." Her story began to make headlines everywhere. She couldn't pick up a newspaper or watch the news without their theories blaring back at her, but she used every opportunity she could to get Benny's picture out to the public. Everyone wanted a suspect, a face to the monster who would ruthlessly steal a child from his bed in the middle of the night. People were looking for someone to blame, and no one was above suspicion. Every face was a potential culprit, and no one felt safe any longer.

A local television station offered to put up a larger reward for Benny's safe return in exchange for an exclusive interview with Lauri. She couldn't deny the offer. More money could certainly help provide leads to her child and possibly bring forward his kidnapper.

"I don't want her doing that interview," Detective Nelson told his partner, John. "We don't want her saying too much in case the kidnapper is watching. They tend to watch the news and keep up on the investigations so they can stay one step ahead of us."

"We can't stop her from doing it," John replied. "The large reward could help us."

"Well, let's hope it does."

Chapter 3

Lauri sat in the airport, anxiously awaiting the arrival of her mother and sister. She found it nearly impossible to focus on the words in her book with the constant feeling of eyes on her. Discreetly, she looked up to assess her surroundings and soon caught a peek of a man observing her from a few feet away. He was professionally clad in navy blue slacks and a tie, and he was easy on the eyes, but his obvious gawking made her uncomfortable. He glanced at her almost as if he knew her somehow, and it troubled her that he wasn't even discreet with his stare.

"What is his deal?" She asked herself, wondering if perhaps he recognized her from the news. Lauri found his gawking to be exceptionally rude and awkward. She modestly returned to her book but felt his stare persisting. Eventually, he made his way over to greet her.

"Sam," was all that he said as he took a seat next to her. Her nerves were rattled by the stranger. Since Benny had gone missing, she couldn't trust anyone, and she felt extremely uncomfortable. Lauri breathlessly tried to keep her composure as she responded with suspicion.

"Excuse me?"

"I thought you might want to know my name," he replied lightheartedly, in search of her smile.

"I don't," she replied icily, without even giving him a glance. She kept her eyes glued to her open book but couldn't concentrate on the words.

"Really, because I could've sworn I saw you making faces at me from across the room." His lighthearted humor was a breath of fresh air for her and she chuckled, but she wasn't in the mood for small talk or being hit on by the stranger.

"I'm just trying to read my book," she told him with her eyes still focused on the pages.

"Oh, okay then. I'll just sit here and be quiet so you

can do that." He sat back in the plastic chair with one leg crossed over the other and his arms folded.

"Thank you," she said but she couldn't concentrate on the words in front of her. His faint breath on her bare skin forced her attention back to him. She glanced over to find him reading over her shoulder, and it made her edgy. "What are you doing?"

"Oh, sorry," he apologized. "Am I bothering you? I just thought that, well since I'm sitting here doing nothing, I might as well read along with you." The man's behavior was strangely childlike to her, but she didn't feel threatened at his attempts to be charming.

"I'm Lauri," she politely spoke.

"Ah, well, it's very nice to meet you, Lauri," he said. "I saw you sitting here, all alone, so I thought that I would come over and beg you to keep me company until my brother's plane arrives. I can't really be trusted on my own so I'm glad you didn't leave me here to talk to myself, not that your book isn't interesting." Lauri couldn't deny her intrigue in the tall, dark-haired stranger, but she wasn't in the mood for his company or his charm.

"Okay, I see what you're doing here, and I don't mean to be rude, but I just want to read my book," she told him.

"Ah, well, I guess I can't blame you for that. I mean, you shouldn't talk to strangers anyway, right?" He said. "I'll just have to go back over there and talk to myself." They both smiled as he added, "it was really nice meeting you."

Lauri shook her head with a giggle when the man returned to his seat and began loudly and unashamedly talking to himself about her book.

"Okay, okay," she surrendered after more than five minutes of his antics. She closed her book with a sigh and motioned him back over.

"Thanks for saving me from that guy over there

who talks way too much," he joked, "but please, try not to flirt with me because I just don't have time for a relationship right now."

"Pouring it on a little thick, aren't you?"

The two strangers sat, lightheartedly chatting while waiting for their relatives to arrive. Sam seemed to be more interested in finding out about her than talking about himself, but Lauri was cautious about offering information. When the plane carrying her mother and sister landed, she politely exited the conversation to greet them.

"Lauri," he called out, catching up to her. "Here's my number. I hope that you'll use it sometime." She left him with a smile but no intention of speaking to him again. Her son was her focus.

"What was that all about?" Her younger sister, Lana, asked.

"Oh just some lonely guy trying to put the moves on me, I guess," Lauri answered. "It doesn't matter because that is the last thing on my mind."

"How are you, honey?" Her worried mother inquired with her arm around her, noticing that her daughter looked like she hadn't been sleeping, and that she had lost weight from the stress.

"Like a zombie stuck in a nightmare," she replied with a sigh. "I'm just glad you are both here." She hugged them both and proceeded through the airport. Having her family there was a tremendous comfort in such a difficult time. She needed the support more than they realized.

"I still can't believe that this is happening," her mother remarked when they sat down in Lauri's living room. "The police still have no leads?"

"None that have panned out, and it feels more and more like they're just accusing me rather than really looking for Benny at this point," Lauri replied. "I just feel so lost." She battled the tears that, yet again, threatened her eyes. After so much crying, she was amazed there were any tears left to shed. She led the women to the back of the house, where the window that had been broken was covered with plywood.

"Who would do such a thing?" Her mother remarked between sobs, and seeing her mother cry intensified her pain even more. "Who would be so brazen?" She hugged her daughter as they cried.

"We are going to find Benny, no matter what it takes," Lana assured her. "We are. We're going to find him, sis. We just need to keep praying and keep the faith." Lauri hoped she was right. She didn't know how long she could go on not knowing where he was or what was happening to him. The women retreated to the kitchen for a snack. "The interview sounds like a good idea. The more people that see Benny's picture the better, and the reward could bring more leads."

"I agree," their mother added. "It certainly can't hurt. I think that we should get you a lawyer if the police suspect you." Laurie had always felt that retaining an attorney would make her look guilty in her son's disappearance, but she agreed that she probably needed one.

It helped her to have her mother and sister in the desolate house, where Benny's absence was so evident. Most nights, it was the last place she wanted to be, but she refused to leave in case Benny made it back or whoever had him tried calling her. Having the companionship of other people in the house made her nights feel a little more secure. The break-in had left her traumatized, and she feared another one. She lay in her bed every night, listening closely for sounds in the silence of the night, someone who might be returning for her. She couldn't rid herself of the feeling of being watched, of being violated by whoever it was that had come into her home and stolen her child. Her brief bouts of sleep were always interrupted by violent nightmares.

With no viable leads and no other suspects, Detective Nelson began focusing more on Lauri, checking her criminal background, her employment history and her previous relationships.

"Well well, what do we have here?" He remarked, staring at his computer screen. "Looks like the devoted mother has an arrest record." His intrigued partner walked over for a look while taking a bite of his sandwich.

"Assault and battery, but that was fifteen years ago," John responded.

"It's still an arrest for violence. Let's pull the record for details, and then we'll get her back in here for another interview." A short time later, they reviewed the details of Lauri's arrest.

"It was an altercation with another girl while she was in college," John explained. "Both girls were arrested." Detective Nelson stared off into space, in deep thought, as he often did.

"She's looking more suspicious by the day," he replied, puffing on his cigarette. "We have no suspect description, no fingerprints or physical evidence, a life insurance policy that she took out on the child and now an arrest for assault." His eye held the twinkle of another case being cracked.

"Still, none of that proves guilt," his partner debated.

"No, it doesn't prove, guilt but it certainly does imply the possibility, a motive." Detective Nelson countered. "I think we have a suspect." John took a deep breath of uncertainty.

"So when do we call her back in here?"

"After her interview with the television station," he responded. "I want to see if her story changes. People in these situations often seem to suddenly remember details differently after a period of time."

The next day, Laurie and her mother approached the

seven story brick building and entered the doors of etched glass. Shimmering, flawless maple floors and art-filled walls greeted them as they glanced around in awe at their extravagant surroundings in the massive lobby.

"Wow! This guy must be some lawyer," her mother stated.

"He's supposed to be the most respected in the county." They rode the elevator to the third floor and followed the signs through the maze of hallways. *Matherson & Paulie*, the stylish lettering on the glass door read. "This is it," Lauri told her mother.

"He's just finishing up with another client," the smiling receptionist informed. "Please, have a seat. He should be just a few minutes."

The women sat on a brown, leather couch while they waited for the attorney to meet with them. Lauri caught glances of the middle-aged receptionist's suspicious stare several times. The media had painted her a suspect of her missing child, and it appeared that the town knew her as just that. She felt accused by everyone around her. The only ones who believed her were her friends and family.

"Mr. Atkins will see you now," the receptionist said.

The spacious, corner office was bright and smelled of vanilla from a candle warmer on a stand nearby. Several plants sat in the window sill and inspirational photos and pictures accented the walls. On one wall, a flat screen television hung and above the door, a small basketball net was hung, like in a child's bedroom.

"What a great office," Lauri thought. She and her mother sat in the leather chairs in front of the attorney's oversized, cherry desk.

"Nice to meet you ladies," the tall, gray haired man stood and greeted with handshakes. "Ms. Felder, I've obviously heard about your case in the media, and I've read the police report." He appeared aloof and unsympathetic as he skimmed through the folder on his desk. With a sigh, the attorney removed his glasses and looked at the women. "I have to be honest here. I don't think I can be of help to you. There just doesn't appear to be much evidence in your favor and, quite frankly, I'm not certain that, given the circumstances, I could offer a proper defense." Lauri's heart fell to her stomach. "My apologies for being so direct about that, but I'm sure that you'd prefer an attorney that could work more efficiently in your behalf."

"With all due respect, Mr. Atkins, I'm being accused of a crime I didn't commit," Lauri crossly rebutted. "Now, I know what it looks like. I can see it in your face that even you believe it, but I'm telling you that I would never do anything to harm my son. He's everything to me and I need to find him. Someone broke into my home and took him right out of his own bed. Don't you understand that?"

"But who would do that?" The attorney pondered. "What reason would they have had? You don't have a lot of money, you're not a public figure, you have no enemies..."

"People kidnap children every day for all kinds of horrible reasons and that's what I'm afraid of, sir. I need help. I can't find him if I have to spend all of my time proving my innocence. Now, I'm willing to take a lie detector test or whatever I have to do. Please, I need your help."

He glared at Lauri with a deep breath and his chin resting on his interlaced fingers as if reconsidering his decision.

"I'm sorry, Ms. Felder, but I just don't think I'm the right attorney for this case." In the week that followed, three more attorneys rejected her also, and her hope was beginning to fade. It was discouraging for Laurie to know that no one, aside from her family, believed her. The town had already made their own assumptions.

"Why would anyone look for Benny when they already see me as guilty?" She asked herself. "How can I prove my innocence and get the help that I need?" She decided that she would do the television interview to explain her innocence and beg for her son's return.

Chapter 4

Later that day, the phone rang.

"I've been waiting by the phone for a week for you to call me but, when you didn't, I figured your phone must be broken," the male voice joked.

"I'm sorry, who is this?" Lauri probed curiously.

"Oh, see, now I'm hurt," he answered. "After our heart to heart talk in the airport, now you don't even know me." Lauri giggled, again amused by his antics.

"Sam?"

"Aha, you remember me after all."

"How did you get my number?" She found it a little strange for him to be calling her.

"Phone book," he answered. She didn't remember even telling him her last name but she must have, she thought. "I'm calling to beg you to have dinner with me." Lauri was flattered, and under other circumstances, she would graciously have accepted his invitation, but the only person that she could focus on was Benny.

"I really appreciate the invitation, but I just have a lot of personal things going on right now," she told him and apologized.

Unwilling to give up, he said, "It's just one dinner. You have to eat, right?"

"Yes, but I just don't…"

"Listen, on a serious note, I'm not out to pressure you into anything or get anything out of it," he said. "I truly just thought we could have a nice dinner with some intelligent conversation and then go back home to our separate houses. That's all. I promise."

Lauri didn't see the harm in one dinner but she knew that it wouldn't stop there. He might have wanted to see her again, and she had no interest in dating. She needed to focus on finding Benny, and she didn't want to involve Sam, but it appeared obvious that he would persist in seeing her. With no excuses left, Laurie reluctantly agreed to dinner, but none of it felt right to her at all, and she considered canceling.

They met at a local Italian restaurant in town, and she was grateful that it was only a few miles from her house. Lauri didn't feel up to socializing and just wanted to politely get the dinner over with quickly.

"If he knew why then he would understand," she thought.

"I'm glad that I could convince you to join me," Sam, as dashingly dressed as the first time she had met him, told her with piano music filling the background. "I hate eating alone."

"Well, I'll apologize to you ahead of time that I probably won't be the ideal dinner companion. My mind has been consumed with other things lately," she explained. "I'll do my best not to let it ruin the occasion though," she added with a smile but was overwhelmed with guilt for even being there. Lauri didn't care about Sam or being out with him. If anything, she thought, the dinner was a big waste of time. She had made her place by the phone in her home, in case there was any news about Benny, but her mother had insisted on her getting away from the house for a little while.

"I've heard that I'm a pretty good listener and confidante," Sam told her with a genuine grin.

"Well, thanks, but it's just kind of personal," she replied with a grim smile while thinking, "as if I would confide anything into this stranger."

"I understand, and thank you, again, for the pleasure of your company this evening," Sam responded with a charming smile. Lauri couldn't help noticing how striking it was. His smile made her comfortable. "So, shall we start with some wine?" She knew that it wasn't a good idea but, with all that had been going on, Lauri saw no harm in one glass to help her relax.

"Okay," she hesitantly agreed.

"You have a beautiful smile," he said with his eyes fixed on hers. "It's nice to see." Though she was flattered, she had no interest in anything other than finding Benny, so she deferred their conversation to a lighter topic.

"So, what do you do for a living?" She inquired.

"Change of subject, huh?" He grinned. "Okay, well, I'm in real estate, nothing exciting about that. How about you?" The conversation always seemed to focus on Lauri, and it made her wonder if he had something to hide.

"Advertising," she answered.

"Well, it sounds like we make a good pair," Sam said while refilling her wine glass.

"Are you trying to get me drunk, Sam?" Laurie joked, beginning to loosen up during the meal. She had to admit that she was enjoying herself. It felt good to take her mind off of everything briefly. "Thanks so much for dinner this evening, but I really do have to go after this."

"What would you say if I asked to see you again?" Sam inquired. Under normal circumstances, she would have been thrilled to, but she couldn't even think about dating with her son missing.

"I don't know. I'd probably say no, not right now, at least," she sighed. "You seem like a really great guy. I just have so much going on in my world right now that dating just isn't on my list at this point."

"Forgive me, Lauri, but I'm struggling to understand what it is that is so consuming. I can't help but develop a complex, feeling like it's just me that you're not interested in. I enjoy your company and I'd really like to see you again, even if it's just as friends."

She bowed her head, staring at her lap. As much as she wanted her life to be private, Lauri felt that she owed Sam an explanation. She broke down and told him about Benny's abduction.

"All you have to say is that you don't want to see

me again," Sam responded in disbelief of her story.

"It's the truth, Sam," she sobbed. "My son is missing." It surprised her that he hadn't already heard about it, given all of the media attention that it was receiving. He reached out his hands across the table for hers.

"I'm so sorry. Let me help you." Hesitantly, she put her hands in his.

"Thanks, but I don't want to involve you. Besides, the media and everyone else in this town already think I'm guilty. Don't involve yourself in that."

"I'm already involved," he insisted. "You just don't strike me as someone who would do something like that."

"I'm not someone who would do something like that," she replied. "I would never hurt my child. I love him more than anything else in the world and, without him, I just sort of feel like I'm walking around aimlessly. I can't focus on anything but finding him."

"I understand completely," Sam told her. "It sounds like you could use another friend so I'm here for you."

"Thank you. I appreciate that," she said, "but now you see why I'm so distant. I don't mean to be. It's just that my son is literally my only priority right now.

"I don't mean to offend, but may I ask where his father is?"

"He's actually in prison, but it doesn't matter anyway because he's never been around," she explained.

"That's really a shame," he replied. "I would give anything to have kids." Sam asked a few more questions about Benny, but Lauri quickly changed the subject, unwilling to give out any more information. He seemed nice enough to her but he was, after all, still a stranger.

"I'm sorry to rush off, Sam," she said after dinner, "but I need to be getting back home."

"I understand," he replied, escorting her to her car. "You know, I meant what I said about letting me help. I hope you will." She smiled and said goodbye.

Reluctantly, Lauri returned to work the following week, and her days were an endless cycle of agony without Benny. All that she had left to live for was her hope that he was still alive and safe and that she could bring him home. The leads were less and less each day but Lauri refused to give up hope. It was difficult for her to understand how, out of the billions of people in the country, no one had even spotted her son, but she was sure that someone would eventually. It would only take one reliable lead, she thought. At the office, Lauri was no benefit to anyone. Her missing child plagued her thoughts with a blend of hope and dread, and she couldn't focus on anything else. Her boss and coworkers appeared to sympathize with her and picked up the majority of her duties.

"Any news?" Lauri's concerned boss queried.

"Not yet," She answered woefully. "I hope some comes soon. I don't know how much longer I can do this."

"I can't imagine how excruciating all of this must be but know that we all support you and we're praying for the best."

"Thank you. That means a lot to me," Lauri replied.

The nights in the empty house haunted her with its silence. Those were the times when she missed Benny the most. She tried watching television or cleaning to keep her mind off of her son but nothing helped. He was gone and she was alone. She often spent hours just sitting in his bedroom, praying for his return. It lent a bit of comfort to be there, where he loved to play. The Xanax that her doctor had prescribed was all that helped her sleep, and not a night passed that she didn't cry for Benny while she slept with his favorite stuffed animal to keep the scent of him close to her. Each morning was a new struggle to face the day, and it was only the hope of finding her child that forced her out of bed. She was barely coping but unwilling to give up.

Lauri maintained continuous contact with the

investigators handling her case. Every conversation with Detective Nelson left her frustrated with the feeling that the police had given up on the search for Benny and had turned their focus to accusing her. She demanded answers but got none, and her patience was quickly wearing thin. She felt like she was constantly being put off by the detectives so she headed to the police station.

"I'm sorry, Ms. Felder, but we still have nothing on Benny other than some false sightings," Detective Nelson informed her. "We're still working diligently to find him."

"I don't understand this," she said. "How hard are you really looking? It's been nearly a month since he was taken. He could be anywhere by now!"

"I assure you that we're doing everything we can," he calmly insisted.

"You're not doing enough in my opinion! How would you feel if it was your child?" She was irate about his insouciant demeanor, as if her missing child wasn't a priority to him.

"We are doing all that is within our resources. We have issued the Amber Alert and notified all of the police departments nationwide. Benny's photo is out there and whoever has him can't hide him forever. Someone will spot him. It's just a matter of time," he told her.

Lauri held her head in her hands and cried. "We don't have time! Please, this is my baby, my whole world, and I can't breathe without him."

"I promise you that we won't give up," the investigator said in consolation. "We will pursue every lead. We'll keep searching."

His words still weren't enough for her. She needed his promise, his vow that her son would be found. She needed to hear the confidence that the detective was unable to give. Lauri was worried about her son, his safety and wellbeing. There was no one else in the world who loved him as much as she did, but she hoped that whoever had him would at least care for him and keep him safe. So many scenarios swarmed her mind. Did the kidnapper still have him? Was he still alive? Was he somewhere nearby? She was infuriated that someone else had taken Benny away from her, and she wished that the abductor would call. She was desperate to know where he was and what he was doing. She needed to know if Benny was content. All she could picture was her son scared and pleading for her, and it was the worst feeling in the world. She wanted Benny to know that she loved him and would never stop looking for him.

Lauri's mother and sister were calling every day for updates and to check on her wellbeing.

"We hate that you live so far away and that we can't be there with you," her mother said.

"I know, Mom, and I understand." Her family realized how much she was suffering and they felt helpless. She carried the weight of the world on her shoulders and there was nothing they could do but offer their love and support, but it comforted them to know that she still had her friends there.

Two days later, the television crew was invited to Lauri's house for the interview. In exchange, the station offered a $5,000 reward to the public for information leading to Benny's return, which they hoped would reel in some new leads or urge someone who knew something to finally come forward. Lauri sat, unnervingly, with the camera and lights on her. She trembled with nervousness and sweating palms as she prepared to answer the interviewer's questions, but she found it nearly impossible to look into the camera.

"Okay, Lauri, just try and relax, and I'll try not to be too personal with my questions," the interviewer told her. "Just remember that we are doing this for Benny." Lauri took a deep breath and nodded in agreement.

The interview began with the reporter giving a brief

synopsis of the story. The questions that ensued were general with regard to what happened on the night of Benny's disappearance.

"I tucked him into bed at nine and went to bed about an hour later," Lauri began with a shuddering voice. The next thing I knew, I was awaken by the sound of breaking glass. I knew someone was in the house so I called 911."

"Could you hear Benny in his room?" The reporter asked. "Was he crying or screaming?"

"No, I didn't hear him at all, so I crept out of my bedroom to get him, but he was gone. No one was there and I thought he was hiding at first, but a rear window in the house was broken and he was nowhere to be found. I just wish I would have gone in there before I did. I wish I would have gone into his room right away, before even calling 911. I would just do it all differently if I could."

"What was your reaction when you realized that he wasn't in the house?" The reporter probed.

"I was panicked, of course, terrified," Lauri responded. Whoever was in the house had obviously taken him." Lauri sobbed through her answers as she was forced to relive the worst moments of her life. She could hardly breathe as she described the feeling of finding that her son had been abducted.

"They were gone by the time the police arrived."

"Yes, she confirmed."

"Do the police have any leads in the case?" The interviewer asked her.

"No, not at this time, and we need anyone who knows or has seen anything at all to please call if you have any information at all, even if they feel that it's insignificant. Every single piece of information matters."

"I'm going to get a little more personal now, Lauri," the reporter warned and, after a brief pause, she asked, "Is it, in fact, true what the media is putting out there, that you are being considered a suspect in this case?" Her compassion was evident, even as blunt as her interrogation was.

"Good question," Lauri thought to herself. She felt like she was their only suspect and was unsure how to answer. She decided to play it safe. "They are interviewing everyone who has had any connection at all to Benny, but no one has been charged."

After a few more questions, the interview concluded with Lauri pleading for the kidnapper to return Benny while the reward flashed over his photo. When the camera turned off, the heartbroken mother dropped her head and cried.

"I know that was extremely difficult, but I really appreciate you speaking with me," the interviewer told Lauri. "I truly hope that this brings Benny home."

Over the next few days, a flurry of phone calls infiltrated the police station, all possible sightings of Benny. Detective Nelson and his partner, John, were investigating each one closely as Lauri and her family prayed for it to be him. When her phone rang, she ran to answer it with the hope of good news.

"I saw your interview," Sam spoke. "You did great. You really held it together for your son."

"Thank you," Lauri answered in disappointment that it wasn't a call about Benny being found. "There have been some possible sightings so keep your fingers crossed."

"You know I will, sweetie, and I'm calling to see if you would kindly join me for lunch."

Lauri preferred to stay by the phone but reluctantly agreed to go. She stepped out the front door and fought her way through the same crowd of reporters that had been there for weeks, once again badgering her with questions as they impeded her walk to her car.

"Thanks for coming," Sam greeted her with a kiss on the cheek. "I know how you hate leaving your house with all that's going on."

"It's so hard to explain, but it's like I can't breathe. I don't know what to do without my son." Lauri couldn't put into words the agony she was feeling.

"It must be unbearable for you. I'm here to help in any way that I can," he said. "The police have no suspects?"

"No, well, none other than me, apparently," she replied.

Sam's eyes grew larger. "Why would they suspect you?"

She sighed with desperation. "I think it's just that they don't have anyone else. I'm cooperating fully but sometimes, I just feel like they are more focused on making me a suspect than finding my child and it's frustrating, you know?"

"I can't even imagine what you are going through," Sam told her. "I'm so sorry."

"No, Sam, I'm sorry for downloading my problems on you, but I do thank you for being a friend. They're pretty rare these days. I don't know who I can really trust anymore. Now, I'm sorry to eat and run but you know I have to get home."

The following week, Detective Nelson summoned Lauri to the police station. Since he didn't offer any information on the telephone, she trembled, only able to imagine the worst.

"No," she told herself. "They have him, and I'm going there to get him." She tried her best to remain positive, but the detective's usually stony face told a story of grief and sympathy.

"Let's go sit down," he told her as the panic sent her heart racing. It couldn't be good news that she was about to hear, she thought as they sat in his undersized office. "The body of a young boy was found this morning," Detective Nelson quietly began as she let out a gasp.

"Oh God, no!" Her thumping heart sank to her stomach and she felt like she would vomit at any second.

"We don't know if it's Benny," he said with solace, with as much sensitivity as he could muster. "The child hasn't been identified yet."

"You need me to identify him?"

"His body is severely burned and he's unrecognizable," Detective Nelson empathetically explained. "Identifying him will require dental records. How soon can you get them?"

If it wasn't for her deep breaths, Lauri swore that her heart would have completely stopped. She could hardly process the detective's words from the sheer devastation that had overtaken her. Her only child could be dead, gone forever, and that had never been a scenario in her thoughts. She felt the life drain out of her at the thought of never seeing Benny again, and she prayed that it wasn't him.

That night, alone in her home, she forced herself to imagine her world without her son. The lifeless house was quiet and hollow. Benny's absence was unbearable to his mother, and the silence seemed to ring out at a piercing volume. All that had gotten her through up to that point was the hope that he would be back, but the thought of him being gone from her life forever made her want to crumble. Without Benny, she had no reason to live. She lay in his vacant bed, still able to smell him and wailing for him. Lauri didn't know how to live without him, no longer able to hug him or tuck him in at night, no longer able to hear his voice or see his smile. She needed him to know how much she loved him. Never had she felt such a loss, and it led her to wonder if it was easier to not know than to confirm the death of her only child.

The telephone rang early the next morning, abruptly awaking Lauri from only a couple hours of sleep. She scurried from Benny's bed to answer it, once again hoping for the best.

"How about breakfast?" Sam asked her.

"Thanks, Sam, but I don't think so," she groggily replied. "It's just not a good day." Lauri felt lifeless and didn't feel up to doing anything or even talking to anyone. Every other day had held a small glimmer of hope in finding Benny, but that day was different. That burned child could be her son, she thought, and she struggled just to breathe.

"How can I help?" Her concerned friend spoke.

"Just pray for Benny," she responded and hung up the phone. She needed to compose herself to make it to the dentist's office for her son's records, but even getting dressed was a tremendous challenge. Lauri had lost the will to live. All she wanted to do was get back into Benny's bed, which, somehow, provided solace in her grief. Being in his cartoon-themed room kept her close to him, and that was where she wanted to stay.

Lauri managed to retrieve her son's records from the dental office with two reporters who had followed her in the parking lot.

"Please, just give me my privacy," she asked of them, but the ruthless media needed their story.

"Has there been a new development in the case?" One reporter probed as his cameraman filmed her.

In her attempt to ignore him, the female reporter asked, "Lauri, has Benny been found?"

"Do you have children?" Lauri finally responded with an icy tone.

"Yes, I do," the woman answered.

"Then try to walk in my shoes for a moment and ask yourself if you would be in the mood to be hounded for a story." Her words left the reporter silent. The other commanded his cameraman to pack up his equipment. Lauri was grateful for their compliance, even if it was only short-lived.

She made her way to the police station with

Benny's dental records, hoping for the best but in disbelief that she was on her way to positively identify a boy who could be her dead son. She was torn inside as to if she really even wanted to know the truth. There was a part of her that would rather retain hope of him being alive than confirm that he was dead. Still, she needed the truth. She needed to know if that child was Benny. Her heart pounded as she tried deep, slow breathing to calm herself.

"Stay relaxed, stay positive," she told herself, over and over. "This isn't him."

At the station, she handed the dental records to the detective, who informed her that he would have the results in the next few days. Lauri knew that those few days would be an eternity to her.

"Hey, Lauri," he called to her as she made her way to the door, and she stopped and turned to face him. "I'm sorry."

"In a new development in the case of five year old Benny Felder, police officials are investigating the burned body of a young boy that was discovered yesterday afternoon," a reporter announced on the evening news. "Detectives in the case are using dental records to determine the boy's identity." Actually seeing the report, hearing those horrible words, crushed the mourning mother, and she fell to the floor in agony, tears soaking her weary, tired eyes. She was living her worst nightmare.

Chapter 5

After a long and seemingly hopeless search, Lauri found an attorney named Ed Ruckerson, who was willing to take her case, even though he, too, appeared a bit doubtful of her story.

"I have to play Devil's advocate and make you see how it may look to some people," the stout, silver-haired attorney told her. "Parents are almost always the prime suspects in cases of missing children, at least until another suspect is identified."

"Do you believe me?" Lauri asked him, staring him in the eye. "Do you believe that I would never have hurt my son?"

He let out a sigh of indecision and replied, "I have to believe you if I'm going to represent you." His face was like stone, cold and unwavering, and she wondered what his true thoughts were. His tone was unsympathetic, almost as if she was wasting his time. Lauri had to admit that he wasn't lending her much faith in him but he was, at least, willing to represent her. She glared into his lackluster eyes.

"I didn't do this," she insisted firmly, "but the police seem to think I did, so I need an attorney who believes in me. If you don't, then please just do me a favor and don't take my case."

"Ms. Felder…"

"Lauri," she said. "Call me Lauri."

"Okay, Lauri, whether I believe you or not, I can assure you that I always give one hundred percent to every one of my clients, and I'll do the same for you." They weren't the exact words that she was looking for, but his promise gave her hope.

The first thing that the lawyer did was contact Detective Nelson to ask if his client was a suspect in Benny's disappearance.

"Not officially," was the detective's response. "We

are still collecting information at this time. It's still an ongoing investigation and no one has been charged." Lauri's attorney then requested a copy of the police report and list of any evidence from the night that Benny had gone missing, and he insisted that any further communication with her be directed to him. The attorney's phone call only fueled the suspicion of Lauri's guilt in the investigator's mind.

"Innocent people don't need lawyers," Detective Nelson told his partner, John, while he scarfed his sandwich. "What is she hiding?"

"She's not officially a suspect," John replied.

"No, she's not," he agreed, "but she is a person of interest, as far as I'm concerned."

"Well, I guess we'll know more tomorrow when we get the results back on the boy," John sighed.

A knock came on Lauri's door, and she opened it to see Sam standing there with a colorful bouquet of flowers.

"I'm sorry for dropping in like this, but I just thought you'd need a friend," he told her, "and I brought you these to brighten your day." He handed her the flowers and a dim smile found her face. Sam seemed too good to be true sometimes, she thought, and she felt guilty for never returning his kind gestures. Lauri began to question why he was choosing to be around her as miserable as she had been over losing Benny. He was an attractive, successful man who probably could have had his choice of women, and she wondered what it was about her that was holding his interest. She didn't feel up to socializing, but felt it rude to turn him away. Reluctantly, she invited him in.

"Sam, you really have to stop this," she warned while walking the bouquet to the kitchen to put them in water.

"No, I don't," he replied with a sly smile. "How are things going? Any news on Benny yet?" He asked her while taking a seat on the couch.

"No, but I did finally find a lawyer," she answered from the other room.

"Do you really think that you need one?" She reappeared in the living room and took a seat on the couch, next to him.

"Sooner or later, yes," she responded with certainty. "I'm not sure that this attorney believes me either, and why should he? The whole town thinks I'm guilty." She dropped her head to her hands. "I just want my life back, Sam. I want my son back." He held her hands in his.

"I'm so sorry," he sympathized. "I'd give anything to bring Benny back to you."

Lauri feared Sam, even as authentic as he seemed to be. After being emotionally and physically abused by her alcoholic ex-husband and authoritarian father, she struggled to trust men. Sam roused her suspicion, in spite of her attempts to see his genuine side. He had an immense interest in discussing her that overshadowed him, and she felt that she knew nothing about him. Their conversations always seemed very one-sided to her, and it made her apprehensive.

In an attempted change of subject, she said, "How about a drink?"

"I could use one."

"Tell me something about yourself," she urged him when she returned with the drinks. "We always seem to talk about me rather than you."

"We do?" He came off as if he hadn't noticed. "I guess I'm just trying to get to know you. I hope I didn't offend in any way."

"So then, it's your turn to tell me something about yourself," she repeated.

"Okay, well, would you like to know how I take my coffee or what I wear to bed at night?" He joked and it provoked a giggle.

"You know what I mean."

"I do," he nodded in a more serious tone. "I'm the younger of two boys, and my family lives about an hour away. I've never been married or had children, but I was engaged several years ago."

"What happened?" Lauri probed.

"I don't know," he said with a deep breath. "I guess, in the end, she wasn't ready to be a wife. She left me standing at the altar."

"Wow, that's tough," Lauri empathized. "I'm sorry to hear that."

"Yeah, I was heartbroken for a while but, you know, you have to pick yourself up and move on. I still have never spoken to her since then so, you see, I'm taking a little bit of a risk chasing you around like this." Lauri snickered at his joke as she dropped her eyes to the floor before raising them back to him.

"Well, you know I have other priorities right now, Sam, but I'm really glad you're here. I do appreciate your friendship." The two of them sat together, talking about Benny. Lauri described her son to him, his generous heart, sense of humor and how intelligent he was. She explained how close the two of them were. "I really miss his hugs," she said with a dim smile and misty eyes. "I miss the sound of his laughter and him saying 'I love you'."

"What happened with his father?" Sam inquired.

"Well, I divorced him when he went to prison for drugs several years ago," she responded. "He was leading another life that I knew nothing about."

"I would say how sorry I am to hear that, but it sounds like you're better off without him. Besides, I wouldn't be here if he still was."

After two drinks, Lauri's words faded mid-sentence as she caught Sam's unwavering stare. She tried to catch her breath as she fought the attraction to him but, when he leaned slowly in to kiss her, she couldn't resist. His kiss was soft and passionate, like silk encompassing her hungry lips. It sent her heart racing and set her soul on fire. For a brief moment, she released every thought and worry in her mind and relished the profound bliss. It exhilarated her to feel the human touch that she'd been missing for so long. Still, Lauri couldn't allow herself to lose control. She had to focus on Benny, and concentrating on anything else would only complicate her life and overwhelm her with guilt.

"Was it that terrible?" Sam joked as she again hung her head.

"No, it was just the opposite," Lauri answered shyly. "I'm sorry," she sighed, guilt- striken. "I'm just…" Sam interrupted her apology to assure her that he understood and that an explanation wasn't necessary. He reminded her of his respect for her, and he insisted that he wanted to be there for her. It felt good to have a friend in the midst of so many accusers, someone that believed in her and her innocence. Trapped in a vulnerable desperation, she succumbed to his kiss, once again, tender and hungry. With her arms latched around his neck, Lauri returned Sam's affection, still illicitly craving more. A stirring need that had been long gone from her suddenly returned and she embraced it. They made passionate love, their bodies yearning the other while tears of pure joy moistened her eyes until she erupted in an ecstasy she had never before felt. For only a second, she loved him.

"Are you okay?" Sam asked with a stare as they lay, face to face.

"Okay?" Lauri thought. "I feel wonderful!" She swore at that moment that her body, clear to her very soul, had just been transformed somehow. But her Eden was soon overshadowed by the absence of her son, and the profound feeling of guilt followed. How could she be so selfish to allow a meaningless pleasure overtake her priority and cloud her focus? She thought. She was shadowed in shame for indulging in her own pleasure.

"There's no shame in this," he told her. "I'm here for you… and with you. I care about you." Lauri was comforted by his words. As she stared into Sam's eyes, she wondered how one thing could be so good in the midst of something so tragic. Maybe Sam was God's way of helping her through her nightmare. Even so, Lauri would have traded anything to have Benny back.

The following afternoon, Detective Nelson and his partner arrived at Lauri's house, and she knew why. Her heart sank to her stomach as the tears invaded her eyes.

"We believe we have a match with the dental records," Detective Nelson stated bluntly. "I'm sorry to inform you that the child is Benny."

She lost her breath and fell to her knees as if violently struck by a freight train. Her world was shattered and it didn't seem real. Lauri struggled to grasp that her only child was dead. She wailed, questioning God for the first time in her life. She was paralyzed with grief, praying that it was only a nightmare that she would soon awaken from, that perhaps there was some kind of mistake. There was no way that she could live without Benny. He was all that she had, and it was an enormous loss for her.

"How can this be?" She wailed. "Who did this?" She asked the investigators. They peered at one another as if searching for words and, without saying what Detective Nelson wanted to, he merely explained to her that they were still searching for an answer.

"We just don't know at this point, but we're not giving up. We're going to find out who did this."

"I need to see him," Lauri said. She yearned to hold her child in a final goodbye. The detective apologetically explained that her request was impossible because he had been so severely burned. "I can't believe my Benny is gone," she howled. Lauri demanded to know every detail of her son's last days, and she pledged revenge on whoever had taken his life. She needed answers. The news was just too much for her to bear, and she began hyperventilating. She couldn't catch her breath from crying, and she began to feel lightheaded. Her chest throbbed with pain.

"Call in an ambulance," Detective Nelson commanded his partner. The EMTs placed an oxygen mask on her face.

"Take slow, deep breaths, okay?" One of them advised while they loaded her into the ambulance.

"All of your tests came back negative," the emergency room physician told her. "I think that you're experiencing a panic attack and anxiety, which is understandable given the circumstances. While a nurse administered a mild sedative for her grief, Lauri's attorney called her mother from the waiting room with the tragic news.

"I'll be on the first plane there," she told him, tearfully.

"She's definitely going to need you," he replied.

With some urging, Lauri agreed to remain in the hospital for the night, where the sedative allowed her to sleep. The next morning, as her swollen eyes slowly opened, the loss of her son once again struck her, along with all of the same feelings, and she felt like there was nothing more to live for. All that she loved in the world was gone and she didn't know how she would survive it. She lay in the hospital bed, grieving Benny's death when Sam walked into the room.

"I heard," he empathetically whispered as he sat on Lauri's bed to console her. "I'm so sorry, baby." He held her in his arms while she cried.

"I don't know what to do," she sobbed. "I can't live without my Benny." Sam lay down beside of her, cradling her in his embrace. "I'm here and we will get through it together," he assured her. "I'm right here."

Lauri couldn't seem to cope with the news of Benny's death, and the panic attacks continued. The nurse calmed her with sedatives and, two hours later, with a prescribed anti-depressant, Sam drove Lauri home.

"I need to go in his room," the grieving mother groggily told Sam.

"I'm not sure it's a good idea right now," he replied, fearing that it would only intensify her sorrow.

"Sam, please, I need to." Lauri slowly walked into Benny's room with a deep breath. The room was pristine with his bed neatly made, still with the sheets that her son had last slept in. "I can't believe that he's never coming back," Lauri said as her tears reappeared. Sam held her as she cried.

"Sweetheart, please, you can't torture yourself like this," he told her. "Let's go into the living room, where you can lie down, and I will make you some tea." He closed the bedroom door behind them and sat in the living room while she slept.

Later that day, Lauri's mother and sister arrived and rushed to console her.

"I'm so sorry, baby." Her sobbing mother held her tightly.

"Who did this?" Her sister, Lana, somberly probed. Lauri sighed, wiping away the tears from her swollen and aching eyes.

"I don't think the police know yet."

Sam politely excused himself to allow Lauri time with her family, and her mother followed him out the door.

"Sam, I really want to thank you for being with my daughter through all of this," she told him. "She really doesn't have anyone here so your friendship means a lot."

"Lauri is a great person so it truly is my pleasure," he responded with a kind smile. He left the house and headed for the police station to see Detective Nelson.

"How is Lauri?" The investigator asked him.

"She's not well at all," he answered. "The doctor has her pretty heavily medicated, and her family is there now. Any more leads yet?"

"No, and just stop kidding yourself. You and I both know who killed this kid," Detective Nelson candidly stated as he puffed on his cigarette. His unhealthy habits and stature made it appear that he could fall over with a heart attack any minute.

"She didn't do it," he confidently told him as he stood with his chiseled arms crossed. The investigator and his partner peered suspiciously at him.

"Oh, come on, Bruce, you're an undercover cop. You know how these cases work," Detective Nelson said. "Hell, you've been investigating her for months. You're the insider here."

"Yes, and as the insider, I'm sure that she didn't do this," Bruce assured his partners.

"Holy shit, you fell for her!" John proclaimed. Bruce dropped his head with a sigh and his partners had their answer. "You broke the cardinal rule."

"Listen, I know that I crossed the line, and I'll face the consequences for that, but I know, without a doubt, that Lauri did not commit murder," he insisted. "I'm positive."

"Okay then, who did it?" Detective Nelson asked him with dubious eyes. "We've got a dead child, damn it, and the only evidence that we have points straight to the mother. You were supposed to get close to her for the proof and, now, you are telling me this?"

"I'm telling you the truth, and I want to find Benny's killer as much as you do, and as much as Lauri does", Bruce argued in the loud tone that echoed the detective's. "You haven't seen the toll that all of this has taken on her."

"Don't blow this, Bruce," Detective Nelson barked. "Don't ruin a good career over this woman. Keep your feelings out of this for now."

"She's a manipulator, bud," John added. "She's telling you what she wants you to hear, but you don't know anything about her."

"I feel like you don't know anything about her, and I'm going to request a transfer off of the case," Bruce replied, walking out the door as Detective Nelson angrily threw up his hands in frustration.

His colleagues were right. Bruce had fallen for Lauri. What began as an undercover investigation to prove her guilt had blossomed into an unexpected infatuation with the woman of his dreams. He had gone in to entice her into a confession by captivating her, only to discover an innocent mother. Bruce wanted to tell Lauri the truth about who he really was but, in her grief, he knew that it was the wrong time. He knew that she wouldn't be able to forgive what he had done. He worried about his career. It would be over if he blew his cover, and especially if he became romantically involved with their murder suspect, even if he was no longer on the case. The crossroads where he stood would determine his future, and his decisions were risky. He wondered if they were worth the consequences.

The day of Benny's funeral arrived, and Lauri wasn't sure that she would make it through. Because the loss had been so difficult, her mother and sister had made nearly all of the arrangements. Lauri was terrified at the thought of the final goodbye to her son, and Lana insisted that she take her medication for her nerves.

The floral-scented funeral home was crammed with friends and acquaintances of the family, as well as people in the community who had followed the story, all who held a sympathetic gloom in their faces. Lauri felt the eyes of each one as she slowly made her way through the crowd, her body trembling and her heart pounding. Their stares were like daggers piercing her, and their whispers rang loudly in her ears. Everyone awaited a reaction from her, but she refused to face the casket that held her son's remains.

"I can't go in yet," Lauri told her mother and sister,

who were both by her side with their arms around her while Sam walked beside them.

"It's okay, honey," her mother consoled. "We're here with you." Slowly, they made their way to the undersized, closed casket that cradled her beloved child. Tears flooded her eyes and her knees weakened as she laid her hand on the polished, gray wood.

"Mommy loves you so much," she sobbed in a soft and trembling voice. The pain that enveloped her body was unbearable as she struggled to breathe. She laid her head on the casket and mourned her son. Never could she hold him again, hug him again or hear his voice calling her again, and it was the most devastating feeling in the world to her. She was living her worst nightmare, and there was no escape from it.

"Let's go sit down," Lana told her as she and her mother, too, wept for the child that had been stolen so tragically from them. Together, they sat, grieving their profound loss with tears and hugs.

It didn't take long for those in attendance to begin approaching Lauri, each offering their condolences, many of them strangers. Whether or not they were suspicious of her, they followed, in numbers, with their sympathy. Lauri did her best to hold herself together while she spoke to people, and they hugged her, but the loss of the person she loved most in the world consumed her. Sam held her tightly as she sobbed.

"Thanks for coming, Sam," she said.

"I wouldn't be anywhere else," he replied sympathetically.

Detective Nelson sat quietly in the back of the room, near the entrance, hoping not to be noticed by anyone. He hadn't spoken to Lauri and wasn't sure if she had spotted him, but he and Bruce had locked eyes. Inconspicuously, the detective observed the people around him, studying their behavior and listening to their words in hopes of additional clues about the murder. Some sobbed over the child's death and some simply shook their heads in confusion while a few whispered among one another about Lauri and if she was truly guilty of such a heinous crime. Detective Nelson watched her closely, analyzing her demeanor with others and her reactions to their words. He watched her interaction with Bruce and he studied Bruce's with her. Lauri's sorrow appeared genuine to him. She didn't seem to be faking her anguish and tears, and it made him sympathetic toward her, but he didn't dare show it. He would have never shown his feelings in any of his cases. His job was to solve them.

The funeral was adorned with prayer and organ-generated music that only seemed to make Lauri's tears flow more fluently. The minister spoke of Benny's smile, his love for football, his favorite cartoons and even his humorous antics were orated to highlight his young life. The memories that rushed through Lauri's mind made her smile amidst her tears. She hoped that her eulogy to her son would be just as expressive to celebrate his perfection. All eyes were on her as she stood at the podium to speak.

"In a world that is so full of uncertainty and hardship, my son, Benny, was my shining light," she tearfully began with slow, uneven words because of her medication. "Even on the worst of days, he made the world better, happier. I will always cherish our times together, snuggling on the couch in front of the television, laughing together as we played ball in the yard or colored in his books, the ice cream sundaes that always completed our Saturdays. I'll never forget how it warmed my heart to hold him in my arms, to hear him say, 'Mommy' or 'I love you', to feel his little kisses on my cheek after a big bear hug from him." Lauri sobbed and sniffled between sentences, struggling to hold back yet another burst of tears. "Our time together was so short-lived, but I will forever hold every single moment in my heart and in my soul, and I will carry him with me always. Benny is still my world, my life and my pride, and he will be missed by so many who loved him. I know that, with God, he is still that grinning and free-spirited child who loved all of you as well. May God bless him and keep him that way," she concluded before returning to her seat and, once again, erupting into tears.

After the funeral, Lauri spotted Detective Nelson and it infuriated her.

"Do me a favor and give me enough respect to attend my child's funeral in peace, without your scrutiny," she firmly spoke when she approached him. "The media was kept out of here and I would appreciate you leaving, as well." Bruce stared as the two of them conversed.

"Ms. Felder, there was no disrespect intended," he told her. "I'm only here to offer my condolences and watch for any possible suspects. They sometimes have a tendency to appear at the funeral services to pull suspicion away from them."

"You mean, you're here to watch me," she rebutted. "I want you out of here right now."

The investigator obliged her request and made his exit. She knew that his true intention for being there was solely an attempt to aid in his investigation. He and his partner had been harassing her since Benny's disappearance, and she felt that both she and her family deserved to have a proper funeral for Benny, without their presence.

Outside, the media filled the parking lot, awaiting the grieving mother to exit the building. She dreaded being hounded with questions from them again, especially after her son's funeral, but they blocked her only way out.

"I'm going to go pull the car up to the door," Lana told her sister. Lauri, Sam and her mother hurried into the car before the reporters could get to them, but some relentlessly followed the funeral procession to Benny's burial site in the cemetery.

"These people just don't give up!" Lana exclaimed with frustration. "How low can you get?" Lauri, with her mother and sister by her side, took their seats next to the casket, beneath the tent while light rain fell from the clouds.

"That is just terrible!" Her mother barked.

"Anything for a story, I guess," Lauri replied as the reporters camped themselves several feet from the service. She was outraged over their behavior as they snapped photos.

"Let me go say something to them," Bruce remarked. He wanted desperately to use his influence as a police detective but decided against it. "Gentlemen," he began, "this is a private service, and the family is insisting that you respect their privacy and leave immediately so that law enforcement isn't necessary." They packed up their equipment and left the cemetery but, on the street in front of her house, a few still remained.

They scurried into the house, locking the door behind them and closing the blinds.

"I'll make us some hot tea," her mother said as the phone rang.

"How's she holding up?" He asked Lana when she answered it.

"Hi Sam," she greeted. "She's doing as well as she can be in this situation. "I know that she really appreciated your support today."

"Could you please tell her that I'm thinking about her and to call me if there's anything she needs?" Lauri appreciated his offering of support. His friendship meant everything to her.

"I just can't believe that my baby is really gone," Lauri sobbed with her head in her hands while the trio sat at the kitchen table, and her mother arose from her chair for a hug. "It just doesn't seem real. It's like I keep waiting for him to run through that door any second, asking me what's for dinner, like he always did."

"I know this is excruciating for you, sweetheart, but Benny wouldn't want to see his mommy hurting this way," her mother consoled. "He would want you to remember the good times and smile when you thought of him. He would want you to carry on with your life. You know that." It was easier said than done. Of all the things that Lauri had done in her life, being a mother was her priority. It was what she lived for in the five years that she had Benny, and she didn't know anything else. She didn't know how to live without him.

Chapter 6

Two days later, the investigators stood at Lauri's front door, and she invited them in.

"Please tell me you have who killed my son," she pleaded. The detectives glanced at each other as Detective Nelson took the lead in the conversation.

"We do have a suspect," he replied with a frigid stare. "You're under arrest for murder, Ms. Felder." Lauri's heart dropped and the world felt as if it had just stopped as she tried to process his words.

"What? No! You've got to be kidding!" she squealed as panic set in. The detective casually handcuffed her.

"What are you doing?" Her sister probed. "Take your hands off of her!"

"I'll call your attorney," Lauri's mother told her.

"I can't believe this!" She exclaimed, and she demanded to speak to her attorney as the detectives led her to their car.

"We'll allow you to call him after you are processed at the station," John told her. Her mind was reeling with questions of why she was being accused and what was going to happen to her. Lauri was petrified, and she knew that she had to make them understand that she was innocent. She realized how the situation may have looked to the detectives, and she needed to a way to get through to them.

Plastic chairs sat in the booking area of the police station, where handcuffed men and women sat angrily and complaining. Some were inebriated with drugs or alcohol, some were sleeping and couple had even been beaten up. An officer at the jail sat her down with them and handcuffed her wrist to the chair. She felt humiliated and diminished, like less than a human being, as she was treated as just another number in their system. Until then, she had never felt any sympathy for people in jail, assuming they deserved to be where they were, but she had just become one of them, and she was sure that what she was accused of was far worse than their crimes. She analyzed her cold and grubby surroundings, the way that the officers spoke to the detainees with no compassion or sympathy. She noticed the pungent blend of body odor and urine. Lauri knew that she didn't belong there, and she would have done anything to run away. She dropped her head and wept.

"This is going to be my life," she thought.

Her fingerprints were taken before a female police officer led her to a small, semi-private area.

"Strip down," she commanded her sternly.

"Excuse me?"

"You heard me. Strip your clothes so I can search you." Her tone was icy and insistent. Lauri had never felt so humiliated as she hesitantly obeyed. The officer sifted through her clothing before instructing her to bend over. "Now I need you to squat and cough three times," the officer demanded and Lauri did, crying all the while.

"This isn't who I am," she told herself. "Why can't they see that I'm not a criminal?" It all felt so unfair and disparaging.

"Okay, put these on." The officer handed her a gray jumpsuit with the jail's name stamped on the back. It made jail feel even more real to her and officially dubbed her a criminal. She felt defeated and hopeless as she sobbed, trying to cope with her circumstances.

Lauri was permitted to call her attorney, who arrived nearly an hour later. They convened in a tiny, block room with a single table. It felt cold and barren to her.

"There has to be a mistake," she told the lawyer. "I didn't do this. I didn't kill my child."

"I'm going to take care of this," he insisted. "We are going to get you out of here, and I'll find out what kind of evidence warranted your arrest. In the meantime, try to stay calm and don't answer any questions without me present."

"How long will I have to be in here?" She sobbed.

"I don't know until I talk to the investigators, but I promise to get you out just as soon as possible," he answered before leaving for his mission.

His words brought little comfort to Lauri as she sat in a tiny, dank cell of painted block and steel. It felt cold and suffocating, as though the walls were closing in on her, and she couldn't stand the thought of staying in there for even another minute. With her head in her hands, she cried and prayed for the truth to come out. There was just no way that she could live that way, behind bars, she thought, especially being innocent. She knew she didn't belong there.

A few hours passed before her lawyer returned and she was relieved to see him, hoping for good news while she held her aching forehead.

"Okay, the good news is that we are bonding you out," the attorney announced, and she sighed a breath of relief. "The bad news is that it won't be until tomorrow." Lauri's hopes were immediately shattered.

"Tomorrow? I have to spend the night in here?" She felt panic taking her over.

"I'm sorry, Lauri. There's just no other option, but I will be here first thing in the morning, when the Magistrate is in, and we'll get you out of here. Just try to hang in there and get some rest if you can."

"Get some rest," she echoed, "not in here." Lauri paced the gray-painted concrete floor of her tight quarters, wondering what to do. "How did I end up here?" She asked herself. "How does an innocent person end up in jail? What happened to innocent until proven guilty?" She had just suffered the loss of her only child and was forced to sit in jail for a murder she didn't commit. She was trapped in a nightmare with no way out. Lauri needed to find Benny's killer but she didn't know how. Her mind reeled with questions about her son's murder and her future. All she wanted was to have Benny back as she lay on the paper thin mattress, in tears. Lauri felt like her life had lost all meaning and purpose, and she wondered why she was being punished. She wanted to close her eyes and awaken in her home with Benny in her arms, or simply not to wake up at all. With her eyes closed, she blocked out her surroundings with thoughts of her son, remembering his smile, the feel of his arms around her. She recalled the sweet sound of his voice calling out to her and the humorous antics that always drove her crazy, and she would have given anything in the world to have it all back again. She was suffocating without Benny. The heartache was overwhelming, and she wondered how she would ever survive the pain. Those prison walls couldn't compare to the prison that she was already living in.

The echoes of thunderous voices and slamming cell doors jarred Lauri from her slumber early the next morning. She had hardly slept. Reality, once again, slapped her in the face as her eyes opened to the metal bars and concrete walls. The little bit of sleep that she had had been her only escape. It was 7 a.m. and time for breakfast, but Lauri's stomach couldn't handle food. She lay on the rigid cot, anxiously awaiting her lawyer's arrival to get her released from jail.

"Hey girl," the young woman who shared her cell said when she received her meal, "aren't you going to eat?"

"I'm not hungry," she replied in her gloom.

"So, you're just going to lie here all day?" She queried, but Lauri offered no response. She didn't care that she appeared to be inconveniencing her cellmate, and she just wanted to be left alone. The girl had been brought in for a drug charge. When she finished eating, she began talking about herself endlessly to Lauri, about her young daughter, an ex-boyfriend, her drug addiction and about her life as a stripper. Lauri couldn't have cared less about the stranger's life and troubles, but she had no choice but to listen to them.

"I really don't like the term stripper. I prefer dancer because that's what I am. I mean, there are girls in the club who don't know how to dance. They are just strippers."

"Your daughter, does she know what you do?" Lauri couldn't help but ask.

"Oh yeah. She jokes that she's going to be a dancer too." The woman let out a chuckle, but Lauri was appalled by her statement. "I do it for her. It's quick and easy money that I couldn't make in any other job, especially if I'm willing to go home with a guy, ya know? My daughter gets anything she wants. She's spoiled.

"Wait, so you go home with these strange men?"

"Oh no, baby, not all of them. There has to be a vibe there.," she said. I'm a good judge of character, so I can tell what kind of guys they are."

Lauri was flabbergasted over how normal the woman made it all sound, almost like it didn't even bother her. It was difficult for her to fathom a life like that, and she felt compassion for her.

"I did stop dancing while I was pregnant and now, I I'm back at it, but it's my addiction that brought me here." It made Lauri appreciate her own life, even with all that she was going through.

Four hours later, she finally walked out of her confines, elated with freedom. Jail was the last place that she ever wanted to be again. She couldn't wait to take a shower and relax in her own home. In the car, Lauri's attorney spoke candidly to her about her charges.

"They've charged you with murder and nearly refused your bond," he explained. "The good news is that they don't have much in the way of evidence against you."

"How can they have any evidence if I'm innocent?" She inquired with concern.

"It appears to be circumstantial, mostly, meaning that they have no other suspect so they are blaming you," the attorney told her. "Those are tough cases to prove but still not impossible. We are going before a jury on your court date but, until then, I want you to be a model citizen, toe the line and, for God's sake, don't leave the state. The prosecutors will be looking for anything that can be used against you in this case."

Lauri was still stunned. The entire situation seemed surreal, like an ongoing nightmare that she couldn't wake from. All that she could do is pray for the truth to free her from the accusations.

A few days later, Lauri called Sam. Her family had gone back home and she needed a friend, someone she trusted to confide in. When she invited him to her house to talk, he sounded distant and hesitant.

"Is something wrong?" She asked him.

"I'll come over so we can talk," was his response, and she knew it wasn't a good sign.

Lauri pondered his demeanor toward her and wondered if he had suddenly lost interest or wanted to distance himself from the stigma attached to her. She worried if he, too, believed her to be guilty of her son's murder. If he did, she couldn't blame him. Even though she was innocent, all those around her were skeptical, at the very least. Lauri didn't want to lose Sam's friendship and she hoped that he believed her, but she understood how her situation looked to those around her. She looked guilty because there was no one else to blame. The police blamed her and the media blamed so why not her community, too?

He arrived with a nervous, dim smile, and the mere sight of him somehow comforted her. Still, he wasn't himself, and she feared their friendship's end. They sat down with coffee as Lauri took a deep breath before interrogating her friend. His distant eyes warned her of more bad news.

"Is there something wrong, Sam?" Lauri probed. "You just don't seem like yourself today."

He wanted to tell her the truth, that he wasn't who she thought he was, that he had been investigating her in Benny's disappearance and that Sam wasn't even his real name. Just the same, he had fallen for her, and he was afraid of her reaction. He felt that she would never understand, nor would she forgive him and, given all that she had been going through, he didn't want to add to her stress. Bruce knew that he had to confess before she found out another way, but he couldn't find the words. He made a decision to play it safe.

"No, I'm sorry. There's nothing wrong," he answered with a reassuring calm. "It's just been a rough week at work, but I don't want to talk about that." He arose to take a new seat beside of her. "I want to talk about you." He warmed the mood with an embrace, and tears saturated Lauri's eyes. Bruce glared at her with concern. "What's wrong, honey?" He knew about her arrest, but he couldn't tell her that. Lauri tearfully explained to him what she had been through with her arrest.

"They treated me like a common criminal, like a murderer, and I was so scared," she told him. "No one believes me, do they?" He was irate with Detective Nelson for his actions, but he understood the procedure.

"Oh, baby, I believe you. Your family and friends believe you because we all know you. We know who you are and know that you could never have brought any harm to your son. I'm so sorry that you've had to go through all of this," he empathized, holding her again. "I wish I had known you were in there." Bruce was sure of her innocence and needed a way to clear her of the murder. He hated lying to her and had requested to be taken off of the case but was refused and sworn to secrecy about who he really was. Blowing his cover would have meant serious trouble and cost him his career. His only way out, if he wanted to be truthful with her, was to quit the department, and it weighed heavily on him. "I'll be here for you," he assured her. "It's going to be okay."

"Sometimes, I feel like you're the only one in this town who believes me," Lauri told him. "I'm sorry that I've never been good company since we've met, Sam. I swear, I really was a happy and fun person before all of this, and I wish you could have met me then instead of during this."

"Hey," he replied, guiding her eyes to his, "I like you just the way you are, no matter what the situation is. I just want to be a part of your life, in whatever capacity that you'll allow me to be."

Lauri gazed into his inviting green eyes that told her he loved her, and she leaned in to kiss him. His lips encompassed hers, like a bed of silk enveloping her body, and they offered comfort. Sam swallowed her in his arms, holding her snugly against him while the passion between them ignited. She craved his touch, his kiss, and she refused to let him go at that moment. Lauri pulled off his shirt for a repeat of their last encounter.

"Are you sure about this?" He queried.

"Yes," she responded breathlessly. "I need you."

"I need you, too," he said, lying down on top of her as they kissed. They took their time with each other, not rushing the inevitable but relishing the solace together. "You're so special to me," he said and they continued to slowly undress each other. His lips grazed her neck and chin while hers caressed his bronze chest. Lauri felt like a teenager again. Bruce breathed life back into her.

"Come with me," she said, leading him into her bedroom. They were barely inside when he grabbed her and kissed her again. She pulled him gently on top of her in bed as their bodies meshed in ecstasy.

"I want you so badly," he told her.

His lips trailed from her neck downward with his fingers ensuing as she whimpered with pleasure. His soft, slow touch drove her wild and left her yearning for more of him. He made his way up and down her entire body and back to her Eden as she arched her back to him. She cried out uncontrollably as he worked his magic until she couldn't take another second and exploded in bliss. Their entwined bodies danced a slow groove of passion and fervor, the two of them savoring every moment together. Lauri needed him. She craved his touch and the security of his arms. She had fallen for Bruce, and he had fallen for her. The attraction was alluring and powerful.

"You're so beautiful," he told his lover as they made love. "You're amazing."

"I need you," she replied as the pair erupted in a passionate delight.

As they lay in their silent paradise, Bruce yearned to tell Lauri the truth about who he was. He felt guilty for living his lie, and he was afraid of her finding out and thinking that his feelings for her weren't genuine. He was afraid of losing her. At that moment, his career as an investigator no longer mattered. She mattered. He knew that if Lauri found out that he was investigating her case, the betrayal she felt would end their relationship for good but, if he confessed, he would be fired from his position immediately. Bruce was left to choose which of the two meant more to him. He gazed into her eyes.

"I'm really falling for you, Lauri," he admitted. "Do you feel that for me?"

"Yes, I do," she replied and she meant it. "You've become so important to me, and you're the only good thing left in my life." She saw apprehension in his face. "What's wrong, Sam?" It appalled him that he had just made love to a woman who he couldn't even tell his real name to. At that moment, he would have done anything for her. Bruce caressed Lauri's cheek as they lay, gazing into each other's eyes.

"I think I love you." He had confessed the words

that terrified him the most because of his fear of her not feeling the same and because it meant giving up the career that he had worked so hard to achieve. Lauri smiled and kissed him.

"I love you, too." If her love for him was genuine the way he hoped, Bruce was going to embark on a career move to build his life with her.

The following Monday morning, Lauri sat in her attorney's office, discussing their strategy for court.

"It is important that I know all that there is to know," the lawyer told her. "The State is going to eat you alive. They are going to portray you as a cold-hearted killer, and they will bully you on the stand."

"What evidence do they claim to have?" Lauri asked him.

"Well, as strange as it sounds, their evidence is actually lack of evidence," the attorney answered, leaning back in his black, leather chair. "In other words, they have basically ruled out the possibility of any other suspects, leaving you to take the blame. We need to prove your innocence. Since there has been so much publicity around this case, I have also filed a request to have your hearing moved to another jurisdiction to better your chances of a fair trial." He appeared worried but hopeful.

"Be honest with me, Ed. What are my chances?" Lauri asked with her arms folded, hoping for good news.

"I'd say your chances are good, but we have to convince the jury. It's all in the presentation when there is no substantial evidence."

The media had been following Lauri since Benny's disappearance. Reporters waiting to pelt her with questions were practically camped out with their cameramen in her front yard and even at her job. She couldn't read the newspaper or listen to the local news without hearing about her case, most of the stories presumptuous and falsified. It was frustrating and, at times, even terrifying. Some were going to great lengths for a story, peering through the windows of Lauri's house, constantly knocking on her door and nearly forcing her car off of the road a couple of times. The reporters even offered her money for an interview, always on the attack with their cameras and microphones in her face. None were welcome, and she continually pleaded with them for privacy. She was forced to keep her doors locked and blinds drawn all hours of the day and night for fear of the media.

"Anything new on her?" Detective Nelson asked Bruce, already aware that he wasn't going to receive much cooperation.

"Yeah, she's extremely distraught over losing her child, as anyone would be. She didn't kill him. There's no way she did it."

"Is that your professional opinion or lust clouding your judgment?" The unwavering detective probed.

"I'm telling you, you've got the wrong person," Bruce insisted.

"I don't think we do," the investigator replied. "Do yourself a favor and take your feelings out of the equation, Bruce, because she's not the kind of woman you can take home to mama for the holidays. She's going to prison for a very long time."

With all of the chaos in her life, Lauri managed to keep working and was grateful for her understanding boss and management. Her coworkers had been lending their support and offering to help in any way possible, and the company had even beefed up its security team to fend off the frenzy of reporters that showed up in the parking lot each day.

"I am so very sorry about all of this," Lauri apologized to them all, guilt-ridden about all of them being forced to endure her turmoil. She wasn't sure if even they believed her but, if they didn't, they never showed it.

It seemed that she couldn't go anywhere without the

bedlam of the media harassing and following her, people staring and whispering and even mothers frantically pulling their children away from her, as if she would harm them. The case had laid a stigma on her and plagued her a child killer and, even if she was found innocent of the charges, she was certain that many still wouldn't believe her.

As Lauri's court hearing approached, the strategy meetings with her attorney became more frequent. She was frightened by the mere thought of reliving her tragedy in front of a group of strangers who would determine her fate, without even knowing what kind of person she truly was. She hoped that they would see the truth, but she realized that it was all about public perception and how her attorney presented her to them.

"I'm not going to lie and tell you that this will be easy," her lawyer warned. "We are in for the fight of our lives here because you have a public who already thinks you are guilty. Those jurors are sworn in as unbiased, but they have still seen the news reports about you and have already formed their opinions about you, so my job now is to make sure that they see the real you, the kind and loving mother who could have never committed a crime like this." The uncertainty displayed on his face made her nervous. If her own attorney wasn't confident, then how could she be, she thought. She was sure that he had faced his own level of scrutiny for even representing her.

Once again, her devoted mother and sister flew in to support Lauri through her trial. They filled her with reassuring and comforting words, and they vowed to stay by her side, regardless of the outcome.

Bruce received a subpoena to testify for the State as their star witness and, though he endeavored to be excluded from testifying, he couldn't get out of it. He hadn't gotten the opportunity to tell Lauri the truth about who he was and he didn't want her to find out through court. Bruce dreaded even the thought of testifying against her, especially since he had fallen for her. He was forbidden to have any contact with her before the trial and he nervously paced the floor of his living room, searching his mind for a way out of testifying. If he didn't show up, he would lose his badge and a warrant would be issued for his arrest. Still, it almost seemed worth it to him. None of that meant as much to him as having Lauri in his life, but he knew that she would never forgive him for his betrayal. The entire situation sickened Bruce. Lauri had made multiple attempts to reach him, and he was sure she was wondering why he had suddenly halted his contact with her, especially when she needed him most. He had even hidden silently in his home a couple of times while she knocked on his door, and he felt shame for avoiding her.

"Sam, I'm not sure what is going on with us," her final voice mail to him said, "but it is obvious that you have disconnected from our relationship. I just want you to know that I understand. I come with a lot of baggage, and I should never have expected you to carry my burdens. Maybe it's better this way since my future isn't clear. Just know that I meant what I said about loving you, and I will always carry you in my heart. Goodbye, Sam." His heart ached from her words, and all he wanted to do was hold her. It tortured him to know that she thought he didn't want her and love her desperately.

With her trial just days away, Lauri grew nervous and riddled with anxiety. Her future and her freedom were at stake and in the hands of twelve jurors who didn't know her or her wonderful relationship with her son. All along, she had remained confident in law enforcement and the legal system, but her confidence had since been shaken. She was accused of murdering her own son, merely because the police had no one else to blame. She was innocent but fearful that the jury wouldn't see it. Everyone seemed to be looking for someone to blame for Benny's death. Lauri knew that she could go to prison for the rest of her life, and the thought of that horrified her, especially knowing that the real killer was still walking freely. She walked into Benny's room and lay on his bed, which she swore still smelled of him. As she clutched his favorite stuffed dog, she erupted into tears, desperately missing her only child.

"I'm so sorry, baby," Lauri spoke to him. "I'm so sorry for letting this happen to you. I was supposed to protect you." She wished so much that she could go back in time. If it were possible, she would have done everything different to keep her child safe. "I wish that you could tell me the truth about what happened." Lauri cried for her son. A knock soon came on the bedroom door, followed by the soft voice of her mother.

"Honey, are you okay?" She asked, and Lauri suddenly took note of the warmth in her voice. She saw the pain in her mother's face.

"Do you want to sit with me?" Lauri asked. Her mother sat with her on Benny's bed, cradling her.

"It's all going to be alright," her mother consoled her but her uncertainty was clear. She had lost her grandson and stood to lose her daughter, too.

Lauri looked up at her. "Do you believe that I'm innocent?"

"Oh, honey, of course I do," she answered with complete sincerity. "You're a wonderful mother who did everything that you could to protect Benny. I know how much you loved him." With a heavy heart, Lauri let out a sigh.

"I'm so scared," she said. "I never once pictured my life this way."

"And I never once pictured not being able to make something in your life better. That's a mother's job and, as mothers, we just do the best that we can, honey," her mother replied. "The hardest thing in my life is not being able to bring your baby back to you," she sobbed as they sat in an embrace. Together they cried, praying for a miracle.

It was 3 a.m. the morning of her trial and Lauri couldn't sleep. She sat alone, in the dark, with only the silence of her thoughts. The grandfather clock in her living room ticked away the minutes of her freedom, and she swore that she heard every one.

"These could be my last hours here, in my home," she told herself, and it felt as if it would kill her. If she went to prison, her entire world would become that world, leaving her home life far behind. The vision mortified her. Her life would no longer be her own, and she wasn't sure that she could survive it. As the thoughts raced through her mind, Lauri considered running away, just getting in her car and driving until she reached a faraway place where she could never be found, but she knew it wasn't realistic. She would forever be on the run, with her guard up. She pondered the idea of taking her life to end her misery. With Benny gone, she felt like she had nothing left to live for. Within a few minutes, she found herself plotting her own death with a seemingly easy and painless pill overdose. Never before had she been suicidal, but her circumstances made it seem practical. She could be with Benny again, and life wasn't worth living without him, in her opinion, especially in prison. Then her mother entered her mind, and Lauri thought about what it would do to her to find her daughter dead, on top of the recent loss of her grandson. Tears flooded her eyes as she realized that she would rather endure the consequences than inflict more grief upon her family. As her eyes grew heavy, Lauri walked slowly through her home, relishing every view, every memory and the feelings that each lent, before snuggling into her bed.

Chapter 7

The alarm buzzed at 6:30 and Lauri's eyes refused to open. Her reality was upon her and she didn't want to face it. Reluctantly, she forced herself out of bed. With only a couple hours of sleep, she was lethargic and would have given anything to go back to sleep and ignore her truth. She made her way to the shower with painful, swollen eyes and a burdened heart, dreading the day ahead. The kitchen called to her with a delightful aroma of coffee and bacon and, clad in her best dress, Lauri made her way to the table to indulge herself with her mother's delights for what she felt could have been the last time.

"Doing okay, honey?" Her mother asked while making her a plate, and she let out a sigh.

"Yeah, I'm okay, just didn't sleep much last night." It was the day of reckoning, and Lauri's nerves barely allowed her to eat.

"Everything is going to be fine today," her sister proclaimed, "and when we bring you back here and this whole thing is over, we'll all go out for a nice dinner." It sounded wonderful to Lauri.

Peeking through the blinds, she noticed the usual group of reporters had doubled, all of them waiting for her exit under a dark and dismal sky, which she felt symbolic of her life. "They're up bright and early today," she said, closing the blinds.

"Are you ready for this?" Her mother asked. "I guess I'm as ready as I'll ever be," Lauri answered with a queasy stomach.

It was 7:30 when the three women opened the door to leave. The reporters swarmed them with the usual pictures and questions, pelting them with questions and camera flashes.

"Lauri, how do you feel today?" One asked.

"What do you think the outcome will be?" Another probed.

Lauri hurried to the car, in silence, while fighting off the mob. The blinding camera flashes pierced the windows as they pulled away, and she watched as they rushed to their cars to follow her. At the courthouse, another mob of reporters awaited her arrival and they surged her at first glance, nearly trapping her in her car.

"Lauri, is there anything you want to say?" She heard one yell. It was a struggle making her way through the crowd of cameras and microphones. The reporters followed her through the courthouse, still bombarding her with questions.

"I'm innocent," she asserted.

She was thankful that the media was not permitted inside of the courtroom as she sat in a small, connected conference room with her attorney.

"Okay, now remember, Lauri, there will more than likely be some offensive and possibly even false statements made by the prosecution today, but you can't react in anger because you'll be playing right into their hands. That's what they want is to provoke you," the attorney advised. "The only emotion that I want you showing is the limitless love that you have for Benny. Let that jury feel the pain of losing a child. They will be looking at your body language and your emotions." Lauri nodded in agreement.

"I'm so nervous." Her hands were sweaty and trembling, and her heart raced as if it would leap right out of her chest. She tried to pace her breathing to slow and deep breaths but it was hardly calming. Suddenly, the tremors controlled her entire body as her anxiety grew.

"When you are up on the stand, be honest and thorough with your answers," her attorney coached.

"Give the jury as much factual information as possible and show them that you are hurting."

"That won't be hard to do," she nodded. "I need them to see that I'm innocent."

"Of course you're innocent. Are you ready to go in?" With a deep breath, she stood and nodded.

The courtroom was silent, aside from a few faint whispers. It felt cold to Lauri with its wooden seats, white vaulted ceiling and oak walls, decorated only with the American Flag and Ten Commandments. Never having been in a courtroom, she seemed to notice every detail from the wood railing and Judge's bench to the stand where she would testify. Lauri stared at the jury box, where the twelve strangers would decide her fate. Her mind played a preview of the hearing with her explaining what happened to a sympathetic jury. The scene then switched to the Judge announcing a not guilty verdict.

Lauri found herself with a slight smile before her vision was abruptly ended by the Baliff's voice announcing, "Please rise." Judge Phillip Holstein appeared in his black robe to preside over the hearing. The gray-haired, older man with bifocals on the tip of his nose held a serious and firm expression on his face. He had a reputation for being a strict but fair Judge who ruled precisely by the law for more than thirty years. "You may be seated," the Baliff then told the courtroom occupants.

Lauri, seated at the defense table with her lawyer, casually glanced at the Prosecutor across from her. She was Olivia DeFont, a highly respected, no nonsense woman in her fifties, who was known for her large number of criminal convictions. Lauri took a deep breath and hoped for the best as her trial commenced.

The Prosecutor rose confidently out of her

chair and began a composed and cool stride near the Judge and jury in her high heels. "Your Honor, members of the jury," she began her opening statement, "we are here today to prove that the Defendant, Lauri Felder, intentionally murdered an innocent and helpless child, her own five-year-old son, Benny Felder." The thin redhead in her business suit paced the floor as the leather of her broken in, black heels squeaked and she spoke with confidence. "We will show how, even after taking her son's life, Ms. Felder not only carried on with her life without remorse, but also collected a substantial amount of money from a life insurance policy. Lauri Felder was a divorced and desperate mother who was struggling financially and looking for an easy way out of debt. She was fully aware of her actions, yet still took her only child's life away for her own benefit."

Lauri couldn't believe what she had just heard. It appalled her that anyone would accuse her of killing her child and especially for money.

"Thank you, Ms. DeFont," the Judge said. "Mr. Ruckerson, any opening statement?" He asked Lauri's attorney.

"Good morning, Judge Holstein, Jury," he greeted with a nod while rising. "Today, you will, in fact, hear a tragic story about a five year old child, my client's only son, Benny. You will hear the grim details of a home invasion and abduction that occurred in my client's home in the early hours of October seventh. On the stand today, you will meet a grief-stricken mother who has lost her heart and soul, along with her child, yet stands blatantly accused of his demise, in spite of the lack of evidence. Ms. Felder is not a murderer, but a victim in this heinous crime. She doesn't want money, your Honor. She wants her son back."

"Will the prosecution call your first witness, please?" Judge Holstein requested, and a police officer took the stand.

"State your name and occupation for the court, please," the Prosecutor commanded.

"Officer Bradley Burrows with the Wood County Sheriff's Department," the young, fair haired man responded.

"What did you discover upon your arrival at the Felder home in the early hours of October seventh?"

"Upon arrival at the home, we found Ms. Felder in her living room, crying and screaming that her child had been abducted from his bedroom. She explained to us that someone had broken a window and entered her home at approximately 3 a.m. and that she was unable to locate her son. Two other officers, along with myself, completed a search of the home and found that a window at the rear of the home was broken from the outside."

"Did the home appear ransacked, or was anything disheveled, Officer Burrows?"

"Not at all," he replied. "Nothing appeared to be out of place in the home."

"And did you, your accompanying officers or Ms. Felder notice anything else missing from the home?"

"No, ma'am. All of Ms. Felder's other belongings appeared to be intact."

"And what was your procedure from that point?" Olivia questioned as she continued her pace.

"After securing the home and our interview with Ms. Felder, we notified our department's internal investigations unit."

"Thank you," she responded with a smile. "No further questions." Lauri's attorney took the floor while Olivia returned to her seat.

"Officer Burrows, I just have one question for you," he began. "Did your department determine that the window was broken from the inside or from the outside of the home?"

"We determined the window to have been broken from the exterior of the home, sir."

"Thank you. No further questions," her attorney replied.

"Will the prosecution please call its next witness?" Judge Holstein requested, and Detective Nelson took the stand.

"State your name and occupation for the court, please," the Prosecutor commanded.

"Detective Frank Nelson, lead investigator assigned to this case."

"What did you discover upon your arrival at the Felder home in the early hours of October seventh?" The detective described a visibly upset woman being interviewed by a police officer.

"There was one window that was shattered. The scene was secure, nothing in disarray, nothing appearing to be stolen," he explained. "Two of the officers were leaving to scan the area for the suspect."

"Was the Defendant able to give any information about the intruder?"

"No, ma'am, she explained that she had been on the phone with a 911 dispatcher, who advised her to stay in her bedroom until it was safe," he answered. "By the time she entered the child's room he and the intruder were already gone. She did mention that she believed there was only one intruder in her home, but she couldn't be sure since she didn't see anyone," he added.

"Were there any other witnesses to this crime?" Olivia asked him.

"The next door neighbor claimed to have heard glass breaking around the time of the incident but didn't see anything," he responded. "My partner and I questioned the neighbors on the block, and no one else claims to have seen an intruder or any other activity."

"Detective Nelson, you mentioned a broken window. Did you gather any evidence, such as fingerprints, blood from the broken glass, footprints?"

"We dusted for fingerprints but came up with nothing. There were no shoe prints, no tire prints, no blood on the glass. There was no evidence at all of an intruder, other than the broken window." The Prosecutor followed with specific questions about the detective's interviews with Lauri, along with her criminal history.

"Objection, Your Honor. That's irrelevant to these circumstances," Lauri's attorney intervened.

"Sustained. Proceed to your next question, Ms. DeFont," the Judge ordered.

"No further questions, Your Honor," she said.

Ed neared the stand for his questioning.

"Detective Nelson, you stated that you found no evidence at the scene, other than the broken window. Can you tell me, sir, if the window was shattered from the inside or the outside of the home?"

"It appeared to be broken from the outside of the residence," the detective responded.

"And doesn't that logic insinuate that my client would had to have walked outside and broken the window herself?"

"I'm not insinuating anything. I go by evidence." The annoyed detective rebutted.

"Evidence," Lauri's attorney echoed calmly. "Well, if that's the case and there was, in fact, no evidence to be found at the crime scene, other than that broken window, of course, how, then, did you make the determination that my client, Lauri Felder, is guilty of the crime?"

After a moment of hesitation and thought, he replied, "There was other evidence outside of the crime scene, which was discovered later in the investigation."

"Evidence, such as what?"

"Well, the life insurance policy, for one. There are also witness statements and such," he responded in a casual tone.

"Witness statements?" Ed questioned. "But you just stated, under oath, that there was only a single witness. Isn't it true that all of this so-called evidence that you claim to have is purely circumstantial?"

"Some of it may be considered circumstantial, sir, but logic is how we piece together our cases" he uttered. Lauri's attorney played the 911 tape for the jury.

"Someone is in my house! Someone broke in. I need help!"

"The intruder is in your house right now?"

"Yes, I'm in my bedroom and I can hear rustling. Please, hurry."

"Okay, stay on the line with me. I have police officers in route."

"I have to get my son."

"Ma'am, I strongly encourage you to remain in your bedroom with the door locked until the police can get there. Ma'am? Ma'am? I think she hung up the phone.

"On that tape, we hear the 911 operator urging my client to remain in her bedroom with the door locked while the intruder was in her home," Ed stated. "Then, we hear my client, Ms. Felder, hanging up the phone, against the 911 operator's wishes, to go to her child. Is that what you heard, Detective?"

"Well, uh, yes," he stumbled, "but..."

"No further questions," Ed said.

The prosecution's next witness was the local medical examiner who had examined the child's body.

"There was blunt force trauma to the head and neck and the body had been severely charred," she testified.

"What was your determination as the cause of death?" Olivia asked.

"It was most definitely a homicide," she concluded.

Lauri sat in her chair with her head down, trying to tune out the sordid details of how her son's life was taken. She couldn't bear to hear the torture he'd been through.

"As our final witness, we would like to call Bruce Evans to the stand," the Prosecutor stated.

Reluctantly, he sat down at the microphone and Lauri held her breath in disbelief. She knew him only as Sam, and she wondered why he was testifying for the Prosecution. She noticed his brief glances at her while she watched with confusion.

"Did they summons him?" She questioned her attorney. "And why are they calling him Bruce?" He sat with shame and remorse in his face.

"Could you please state your occupation?" Olivia began with her arms crossed. He kept his apologetic eyes on Lauri and took a deep breath.

"I'm an undercover investigator assigned to this case," he answered woefully, as if he would erupt into tears.

Lauri thought, for a moment, that she had misunderstood. She couldn't believe what she was hearing. "He lied to me," she told herself. She had never felt such betrayal, and anger fueled her. "How could he do this?" She whispered in disbelief.

"What's that?" Her attorney whispered her upon overhearing her words.

"He pretended to be my boyfriend all of this time. I didn't know that he was a cop," she replied.

"My assignment was to befriend Ms. Felder and earn her trust in an attempt to retrieve any evidence or information about the child's abduction," Bruce testified remorsefully on the stand. Lauri stared at him with disenchantment, shaking her head over his audacity. Their entire relationship had been a lie.

"And were you able to accomplish that?" Olivia inquired.

"Yes, we became very good friends pretty quickly."

"Did Ms. Felder ever have conversations with you about Benny?" The prosecutor probed.

"Yes, several times. She spoke about how much she loved and missed him."

"Did she ever talk to you about the night of the crime?"

"She said that someone had broken into the house during the night. She heard some rustling and called 911 but then put the phone down to go get Benny. When she got to his bedroom, he was gone and so was the person who had broken in."

"Did your relationship evolve into anything other than a platonic friendship?" Olivia asked. Bruce took a deep breath and stared at Lauri with love in his eyes.

"Yes," he admitted softly.

"So, it's safe to say that the two of you were dating and even formed a romantic relationship during the time that Benny was thought to be missing?" It hadn't happened the way that the Prosecutor was alleging, he thought to himself, but it was a true statement.

"Objection!" Ed intervened.

"Overruled, counselor," the Judge responded.

"Yes," he was forced to answer, and he was remorseful. Lauri sat with disbelief, wondering how he could have betrayed her, already aware of how much pain she was in over Benny. She wondered how he could have used her like that, knowing that she had trusted him. His testimony stabbed her like a dagger.

Lauri's attorney stood for cross-examination. "You mentioned, sir, that your assignment was to befriend Lauri. Was it also your objective to woo her into a sexual relationship in her state of vulnerability?" Even though Bruce had anticipated the question, the answer wasn't easily found. It had only been his objective to falsify a relationship. He was supposed to pretend to like her, but he had fallen for her.

"Once again, my assignment was to befriend her. The rest was unintentional," he said.

"Unintentional or unethical?" Lauri's attorney responded.

"Objection, your Honor, badgering the witness," the Prosecutor interjected.

"Sustained," the Judge ruled. "Proceed, Mr. Ruckerson."

"Mr. Evans, did you, in fact, gather any such evidence that my client is guilty of murder?"

"No sir, I have no evidence that she is guilty." Lauri almost found her smile with his redemption.

A couple of character witnesses were called on Lauri's behalf, including her boss, who testified about her good moral character and love for her son, and then Ed called Lauri to the stand. Everyone had waited for that moment, and all were curious as to what she would say. With agony in her eyes and trembling hands, she struggled through her version of events between sobs and crying spells as the jury closely observed her.

"Lauri, can you tell us, in your own words, what happened that night?" Ed queried.

"I was awaken by the sound of glass shattering, and I heard some rustling around in the house. I was terrified, thinking that someone had broken in. I locked my bedroom door and called 911, and then I went to Benny's room to get him, but he wasn't there."

"And when the 911 operator urged you to stay in your room, why did you defy her advice and leave your bedroom?"

"I needed to get to my son and make sure that he was safe," she replied.

"When you walked down the hallway to Benny's bedroom, did you notice anyone still in the house or the broken window at that time?"

"It was quiet, so I thought that maybe the person had left and Benny was hiding somewhere in the house. I was frantic when I couldn't find anywhere and didn't even notice the window at that time. My heart was pounding out of my chest, and I just kept looking for my son. I called his name several times and looked in cabinets and closets. At that time, I was pretty sure the stranger had left but, whether he was still there or not, my priority was Benny. The doors were locked so I didn't think he had gotten out of the house."

"What did you do when you couldn't find him?" Ed questioned.

"I went crazy," she replied. "I ran around the house, screaming his name, trying to find him. I even ran into the garage and outside, and that's when the police showed up.

"How was your relationship with your son?" She closed her eyes and smiled while memories of him flooded her mind.

"He was my everything, my heart and soul." Tears streamed down her cheeks. "We always had the best time together, singing and playing. He was intelligent had the wildest imagination, and I always knew that he would do great things. I loved him more than anything."

"On the night that Benny was taken, can you describe to the court the events that took place prior to you going to bed?"

"There was nothing out of the ordinary. I gave Benny a bath at eight o'clock and gave him a snack. Then he brushed his teeth and I tucked him into bed. I went to my own bed and watched some TV until I fell asleep."

"Do you recall any suspicious people or events in the days or weeks leading up to that night?" Her attorney asked.

"No, nothing." She didn't even need to hesitate.

"Have you ever spanked Benny or hurt him in any way?" Ed asked her.

"No, of course not," she answered. "I would have never needed to anyway because he was an amazing child, very well behaved."

"Lauri, what has your life been like since all of this occurred?" Ed inquired, and she didn't know how to even put her agony into words.

"It's been a nightmare," she answered miserably. My life has been turned completely upside down. I'm not only grieving my only child. I'm also trying to prove my innocence. The media has been stalking me and basically camped out in my front yard for months, and my family is enduring the pain as well. My entire world has become a whirlwind. It's like I'm living a nightmare that I can wake up from."

"Did you commit this crime?"

"No, absolutely not. I loved Benny with everything that I had. He was my whole life, and I would never have hurt him for any reason. It's so hard to live without him." She broke down on the stand as the occupants in the courtroom watched, in silence, with sympathy in their faces.

"Since Benny's death, have you made any major purchases with the money that you received from his life insurance?"

"Just his funeral expenses," she answered solemnly.

The Prosecutor stood with an icy stare and her arms crossed, to question Lauri.

"Ms. Felder, you claim that while you were locked in your bedroom, you heard what sounded like a rustling from an intruder. However, if you saw no one or heard any voices, how did you arrive at your notion that there was only one, as opposed to more than one invader?"

"It was only an assumption," she answered. "It just sounded like one person but obviously, I don't know for sure how many there were."

"I see, and in the midst of this rustling noise, you didn't hear Benny at all? No crying? No screaming?"

"No, ma'am, I didn't, but I was also on the phone with a 911 operator."

"Do you find it odd that a stranger grabs your five year old child in the darkness after a window is broken a few feet away from him and he doesn't make a sound?" Olivia probed. "One could almost assume that he knew the kidnapper."

"Objection!" Ed stood to intervene.

"Sustained," the Judge replied. "Please, refrain from assumptions for the remainder of your questioning." Olivia nodded and interlaced her fingers.

"With all of this rustling going on, in the darkness nonetheless, not one thing in your home was in disarray?"

"I can only guess that nothing was moved," Lauri's frustration with Olivia was rapidly growing as she coached herself to remain calm. "I'm not sure exactly what the rustling was from."

"So, you want the jury and this court to believe that an intruder came into your home, found his way around in the dark, with no light, without messing up anything in the home and, meanwhile, snatched Benny before getting out, and all of this occurred so quickly, neatly and methodically?" Lauri realized how it sounded.

"I leave a small light on in the kitchen, and my son had a night light in his room, so it wouldn't have been pitch black," she replied. "The person would have been able to see."

"You also claim, Ms. Felder, that, when you were searching for your son, you did, in fact, go outside, right?"

"Yes, I went everywhere looking for him."

"So, you would have had the opportunity then to break the window from the outside, if you wanted to."

"I didn't…"

"Ms. Felder, may I ask if the child's father was involved in Benny's life?" Olivia probed.

"He's been in prison for the last couple of years and hasn't been involved at all."

"Were you receiving child support?" Lauri knew exactly where she was going with her question.

"Again, he's not involved so, no, ma'am, I wasn't and we do just fine without it."

"So, you were a single mother with no support from the father or family. Am I correct in saying that, financially, you were struggling?" The prosecutor asked, wearing Lauri down, and she expected her attorney to object to the question.

"I worked full time so we made ends meet." Lauri was annoyed at the prosecutor's insinuations.

"Of course." She gave a sarcastic chuckle. "Ms. Felder, is it true that you had an intimate relationship with Bruce Evans?"

"Tread lightly here, Ms. DeFont," the Judge warned.

"Certainly, Your Honor," she responded. Lauri sighed.

"I knew him as Sam, not Bruce. He deceived me into believing that he was someone else and offered support as a friend."

"But you did, in fact, form an intimate and personal relationship with him, correct?" Lauri didn't want to entertain her question.

"Eventually, yes, but…"

"Uh huh, so during this critical period, when you were so desperate to find your missing child, you still found time to date," the Prosecutor sarcastically snarled.

"No, it wasn't like that," Lauri tried to explain.

"Sure it was," Olivia cut her sentence off again. "It was exactly like that."

"You don't understand…" Lauri attempted a clarification but was not permitted to interject.

"Objection!" Ed exclaimed. "Please, Your

Honor." The judge flashed the prosecutor a frigid glare.

"Am I correct that you had a life insurance policy on Benny?" The Prosecutor paced the floor before her.

"I took it out for him last year," Lauri answered, her eyes distrustfully following her interrogator. "Stand still!" She wanted to yell.

"In case something should happen to him?" Lauri was angered by Olivia's implication.

"I had life insurance on both..." She was abruptly interrupted by the prosecutor, mid-sentence.

"But you were also in debt, right Ms. Felder?" Olivia's tone grew louder.

"That has nothing to do with it!" Lauri barked.

"Maybe not, but it sure is a good motive," her voice dimmed with a hint of victory as she eyed the jury. "No further questions, Your Honor." Lauri erupted into tears. She was irate that the prosecutor had so improperly portrayed her to be a murderer.

"The nerve of her!" She thought. She had, somehow, expected more sympathy over the loss of her son.

"Let me hear your closing remarks," Judge Holstein told the attorneys.

"The Prosecution has shown, without a doubt, today that the Defendant, Lauri Felder, is indeed guilty of murder in the first degree," Olivia began. "We have shown that this woman, who has a history of violence, took the life of her only child for financial gain. This crime was very strategically planned, and the murder was intentional and well thought out. She knew what she was doing. There were no witnesses, no fingerprints and nothing in disarray because there was no intruder," she told the jury. "Furthermore, this mother, who was so dedicated to her missing son, began a romantic relationship with an undercover officer, all while pretending to search for her child. Is that behavior typical of a concerned mother? Is it all circumstantial or just a string of coincidences? Ask yourselves, can it bring back the life of this young child?"

Lauri was furious with the Prosecutor for her fabrications about her, the way that she had twisted the events. One arrest, years prior, did not constitute a history of violence, and she would have lay down her own life to save Benny's, but she feared that the jury wouldn't see that. Her attorney stood and faced the jury.

"Lauri Felder is a hard-working, single mother who adored her son," he said. "You heard today from the people who know her what an upstanding citizen and hard worker she is, what a loving mother she was. Not only was Benny, her only child and her soul, stolen from her, but her freedom has been compromised, as well. She has been continuously harassed and grossly accused of this crime since it occurred, before the facts were fully known and before she even got the chance to grieve, so much so that an officer was assigned to spy on her and deceive her in an attempt to get some kind of admission of guilt. No one can give my client back her son, or even a normal life but you, the jury, can give back her freedom and integrity," the attorney concluded.

"Thank you," Lauri whispered to him when he sat down next to her. She prayed for the jury to see the truth but felt that both sides had made good arguments.

Court was adjourned while the jury members retired to begin deliberations.

"So, what do you think?" the disquieted Lauri asked her attorney.

"I would say that we have a good chance. You did well on the stand, and I think you got through to the jury," he said confidently.

"That Prosecutor is a shark. She butchered me."

"That's her reputation," Ed told her. "Don't let her get to you. It's her job to intimidate you and cut you down. She has to create doubt in your story."

The mob of television and newspaper reporters awaited Lauri and her attorney outside of the courthouse, each one yelling questions at her.

"What do you think the verdict will be?" One asked.

"Did you testify?" Another's voice probed.

Lauri made her way through the horde without commenting, her mother and sister by her side.

"You did great, honey," her mother told her.

"Can you believe that Prosecutor?" Lana remarked. "She twisted everything to make you out like some kind of monster."

After his betrayal, Lauri realized that Bruce had been a huge mistake. She felt like a fool for allowing herself to be manipulated so easily, especially when she was so vulnerable and should have focused solely on finding Benny. It infuriated Lauri that Bruce had taken advantage of her, and she was angry at herself for trusting him. Her whole life had been turned upside down and she wondered how she got there. All she wanted was her normal life back.

Chapter 8

Lauri's story was sensational in the nation, and the media was eating it up. Details of Lauri's trial had been leaked and put into newspapers and television reports all around the country in the days that followed her court hearing. Nothing she did was private anymore, and she wondered why, of all of the world's events, she held so much interest. People seemed to thrive on stories like hers and it disgusted her. She had never wanted to be in the spotlight. She had never asked for their attention. All she wanted was Benny back, her life back.

She lay in her bed at night, praying for the jury to see the truth and allow her to maintain her freedom. Replaying the trial, over and over, in her mind, she was furious over Olivia DeFont's allegations and assumptions. She searched for any other information that would have helped her. Lauri thought about Bruce and how he had betrayed her so badly. She had let herself trust someone whom she'd barely known at that time, against her instincts. It enraged her that he had used her, especially to get a conviction in her case. Not only had he hoped for a confession from her, he had taken advantage of her vulnerability at her most fragile time. She was hurt and angry that he had pretended to love her, and she was angry with herself for opening up to him the way that she had, for exposing herself and her feelings so easily. Bruce hadn't attempted any contact with her since the trial, and she didn't expect him to, but part of her demanded an explanation and apology from him.

Since her trial, Lauri was preparing herself for the worst case scenario. She tried to imagine a new life in prison, away from her home and her family.

Part of her wanted to run away to another place, another country where she wouldn't be scrutinized by everyone around her, a place where she could just start over and begin to heal. Another part of her yearned to end her life to be with Benny. She knew that she would never be happy without him. Her life had no meaning without him in it.

Lauri sauntered into her bathroom while the tears soaked her face. She opened the medicine cabinet and took out the bottle of sleeping pills that her doctor had prescribed after Benny's death. The mirror reflected a shell of herself, a wounded soul who had lost her joy and appreciation for life. Taking the pills would finally end her misery, she thought. Her worries would be gone and she would be with her son again. It wouldn't matter, then, what anyone thought. It was an easy decision. Lauri thought of her mother and sister, the only two people she had left in the world. She thought about the pain they would be left to endure from Benny's death, and hers, but they would understand why she did it, she thought. Perhaps they would even be relieved that her agony was gone.

The water from the faucet flowed slowly in the small plastic cup, and she poured a handful of pills into her mouth and swallowed them. Dropping to her knees, she pleaded for God's forgiveness and asked him to reunite her with Benny. Soon, it would all be over, she hoped. Her heart would simply stop beating, and all of her agony would be finally be gone. Lauri returned to her bed, sobbing and praying until she drifted off to sleep.

An hour hadn't passed when her mother arose for the bathroom and decided to check on her. She crept quietly to her daughter's bedroom and peeked in to see someone who appeared to simply be sleeping. Her mother almost closed the door, but an instinct within her refused to let her leave. It led her to her daughter's bed to kiss Lauri on the forehead and it was then that she realized how vague her breathing was.

"Lauri," her mother gently nudged her and felt her skin cool and clammy. Sweat draped her hairline. "Lauri, honey, wake up." When it garnered no response in the lifeless woman, she began to shake her daughter, almost violently, trying to awake her. "Lauri!" She screamed and picked up the phone while her sister rushed in.

"911, what's your emergency?" The operator asked.

"It's my daughter," she responded frantically. "She went to bed and now won't wake up. Help me!"

"Is she breathing?" The dispatcher queried.

"Yes but barely." Lauri's sister began CPR, giving her breaths and chest compressions while the operator remained on the line. "Come on, baby! Don't you leave me!" She wailed.

Within four minutes, she heard the ambulance siren blazing through the neighborhood. Lana ran to the door while her mother took over her attempts at reviving Lauri. Two male paramedics rushed into the bedroom and put an oxygen mask on her while they checked her vital signs.

"Has she taken any drugs or drank alcohol tonight?" One asked.

"No, not that I know of," her mother answered, and she remembered Lauri mentioning her doctor giving her sleeping pills. She ran into the bathroom and saw the bottle in the sink with only a few pills left in it.

"These!" Her mother exclaimed. "They were in the sink and she had a lot more than this."

The paramedics loaded Lauri into the ambulance and began to pump her stomach while speeding toward the hospital with Lana and her mother in tow.

Just as they were pulling into the hospital lot, Lauri vomited and began to awaken, evaluating her surroundings.

"Hi Lauri," the paramedic greeted. "We're just pulling into the hospital, and you're going to be okay. Do you remember what happened tonight?"

"I took some pills," she groggily admitted.

"Okay. Do you remember what you took? Were they your sleeping pills?" He asked her and she nodded.

"At the hospital, she was wheeled into the emergency room, where an IV of fluid was inserted into her arm. Heart and blood pressure monitors kept track of her vitals. Her mother and Lana entered her room and were delighted to find her awake and alert, but she looked clammy and pale with dark circles under her eyes.

"Oh, honey, I'm so glad you're okay," her mother said as she hugged her tightly. "I was so scared." Lauri took a deep breath and peered into her lap with anguish.

"I'm sorry," she replied tearfully. "I just can't take any more." Her mother held her as she wailed in her anguish.

"I'm here for you, honey, and so is Lana. We love you so much, and we will get through this. I promise. Taking your life isn't the answer. Please understand what that would do to us. We're going to get you through this, sweetheart." Lauri nodded, wiping away her tears, but it was much easier said than done.

"I know."

"Please, promise me that you won't do this again." She agreed on a vow that she wasn't sure she could keep but, if it brought her mother comfort, she would have promised her anything at that moment.

Lauri had been in the room, under observation, for a little over an hour when a social worker entered and asked to speak with her privately.

"I'm Paige Daniels," the tall and stunning woman began after pulling up a chair to Lauri's bed. "I wanted to talk with you a little bit and just kind of gauge how you're feeling right now. Is that alright?"

"Sure," she responded but truly didn't feel like talking to anyone at that moment, especially about her feelings.

"Given what happened with you, I want to make sure that you are okay and not at risk of hurting yourself." She bombarded Lauri with questions about her mental and physical health and her home life, and Lauri explained to the social worker why she had taken the pills. "I do know about your story but only from the news reports," the woman informed her.

"My son is dead and everyone thinks I killed him."

"Lauri, I'm not here to judge you at all. I just want to make sure that you're alright and going to be alright when you leave here."

"I'm alright and I do feel a lot better now," Lauri assured her. "I just had a really low moment. That's all. I realize now that that's not the answer and that I would just be hurting the people who love me."

"I'd like to set you up with some counseling to help you through all of this," the social worker told her, "and I'm going to recommend that you stay in here for a day or two, until you're feeling more relaxed and clear-headed. You have a lot of stress on you." A nurse moved her to a third floor, private room that looked out over a lush, green courtyard. A camera was mounted at the ceiling in one corner of the room to monitor her. "We have therapists who work on this floor, around the clock, if you feel like you need to talk to someone," the nurse told her. "She'll be in to introduce herself shortly."

The dimly-lit hallway reeked of bleach and was abandoned of people. Lauri found the silence disturbing but it was the middle of the night. Her mother and sister weren't permitted on the floor except during visiting hours, so Lauri turned on the television and tried to relax. She was almost asleep when she heard a soft knock on the door.

"Hi Lauri. I'm sorry to disturb you. I'm Doctor Phillips," the blond haired therapist whispered. She was stout with a kind demeanor and soft voice. "How are you feeling?"

"I'm okay. Just a little tired," Lauri replied. "Well, that's certainly understandable. You've been through quite an ordeal. We can talk more tomorrow, but I want you to know that I'll be here all night if you want to talk, okay?"

"Thank you," Lauri told her. "I appreciate that."

The next morning, she awoke to the sun peeking in through the window blinds. She could see a few people walking in the hallway and heard the voices of two ladies speaking to the patients. One she recognized as Doctor Phillips from the night before.

"Good morning," a young and bubbly nurse who entered her room greeted. "Would you like to join us for breakfast in the TV room?"

"Um..." Lauri assumed that breakfast was delivered to the rooms. She wasn't up for socializing and just wanted to go home.

"Come with me. I'll show you where it is."

Reluctantly, she trailed the nurse down the hallway to a spacious room at the end. Leather couches and chairs bordered a group of tables in the center of the room, where a few of the patients sat to eat their meals while they socialized, did crafts or watched television. The room was bright and cheerful with inspirational quotes and pictures accenting its walls. "This is Geri, Paula and Reece and over there on the couch are Joseph and Lenny."

"You can sit with us if you'd like," the trio of ladies offered and Lauri wondered how long they had been in the hospital. She didn't really care who they were and wasn't interested in getting to know them because she didn't plan on staying long, but she didn't want to be rude.

"Thanks," she replied while sitting down at the table to join them for breakfast. She felt like a child in a preschool classroom. The women, two teens and lady around her age, stared curiously at her.

"When did you get here?" One of the teens asked.

"About three in the morning," Lauri replied wearily, her eyes burning in the daylight. She wasn't in the mood for their questions.

"What are you in here for?" The teen probed, sizing her up.

"Reece!" The woman with the teens reprimanded. "Don't pry in this lady's business." She gave Lauri a friendly smile and a wink, and Lauri appreciated her halting the interrogation. She wondered if she looked as bad as she felt. The severe pains in her abdomen repelled the food in front of her. All she wanted to do was scurry back to her room, alone, until she was released.

"I'm in here for this," Reece said, showing Lauri her mangled arms. "I'm a cutter. That's what they call me, at least." The teen seemed almost proud to announce her disorder. Both of her arms were masked with slices that she had cut from the elbow to her wrist. Her wounds were incredibly difficult for Lauri to look at. It pained her to see a young girl harm herself that way. She wanted to shake the teen and ask why she would do such a thing.

"You're too young to have any real problems," Lauri wanted to say to her, assuming that she'd done it over a boy or some other superficial reason, but how could she judge someone else when she was there with them, she thought. Each of them was struggling through their lives, for one reason or another, and it didn't matter what the reasons were. They all needed help.

"My father abused me pretty much my whole life," Reece explained. "Nice parenting, huh? He has never even apologized. I guess he thinks it's not supposed to affect me or something. What a joke!" Lauri wanted to cry for the girl who was just sixteen years old.

"Where was your mother, sweetheart?"

"She died when I was eight," Reece answered. "My father was stuck raising me and, when I got a little older, I became more like his wife than his daughter." She explained how she had been forced to assume her mother's role in the household, cooking and cleaning, doing the laundry and catering to her father, by whatever means necessary. Lauri could barely stand to hear another word about the nightmare Reece had been forced to endure throughout her childhood. She couldn't fathom how a parent could do something so horrible.

"I'm so sorry, Reece," Lauri told her. "I'm sorry that no one else was around to protect you from him." Lauri thought about her own situation. "I'm here because my son, Benny, was kidnapped and murdered."

"I've seen you on TV," the other teen mentioned.

"I'm being blamed for his death, even though I didn't do it, so I took some pills last night," Lauri confessed, and the words were as if someone else had spoken them. She had always been far too level-headed to do something so foolish, and hearing herself admit what she had done consumed her with humiliation. "I'm not the kind of person to do something like that. I just... I just broke down, I guess."

"You don't know who did it?" Reece asked.

"I wish I did."

Their conversation wasn't at all what Lauri had expected over a simple meal. She had just met the people that surrounded her and, though she might have once dubbed them as crazy, she realized that they were just people like her, people who needed help with problems that they couldn't solve on their own and, even as tough as it was to confess her problems, she felt better getting them out to someone. She sat with the group for two more hours, listening to Paula, who spoke about her struggle to cope with the recent loss of her husband, and Geri, who battled a drug addiction. Their stories made her look within herself and gain strength from their experiences. She realized that there was hope for all of them. They didn't have to just accept their situations.

Before she knew it, Doctor Phillips was standing at the table with a smile.

"How's everyone doing?" She asked the group before requesting to speak with Lauri alone in her room. "It's nice to see you a little more upbeat today, Lauri. How are you feeling?"

"I'm actually doing so much better today," she responded. "I have to confess how ashamed I am about taking those pills. I guess I just hit my breaking point, but that was really out of character for me. I'm usually very level-headed, and I know better than to do something like that."

"Well, trauma doesn't discriminate," the woman said. "It affects people in ways that they never thought possible and can truly make them desperate enough to consider doing things that they wouldn't have normally done." The doctor spoke with Lauri for nearly an hour before releasing her from the hospital. As happy as she was leave the facility, her grieving heart couldn't bear to leave her new friends behind. They didn't realize the impact that they'd made on her over breakfast that day, in a single conversation. Lauri hugged the three women, encouraging them and thanking them for their words.

"We'll be rooting for you," they told her as she walked toward the door.

Four days after Lauri's trial, the phone rang.

"The jury came back with a verdict," Lauri's attorney told her. She felt her heart fall from her chest, and anxiety swallowed her. They had determined her fate and she hoped that all of the media speculation hadn't played a part in their decision.

The media swarmed her attorney's car the moment that they noticed it and she could hardly open the door amid the mob of cameras and microphones.

"How are you feeling, Lauri?" She heard one reporter ask.

"Do you feel good about the verdict?" Another queried.

Her attorney led her as quickly as possible through the crowd and into the building, where they were prohibited from.

In the drab courtroom that she was becoming so quickly accustomed to, Lauri sat nervously with her attorney, her crossed hands trembling in her lap, her leg bouncing uncontrollably and her racing heart stinging her chest.

"We're here for the case of the State versus Lauri Felder. Has the jury reached a verdict?" Judge Holstein asked them.

"We have, your Honor," one stood to say. She handed the paper to the Baliff, who delivered it to the Judge.

"This is it." Lauri took a deep breath and closed her eyes, praying for a not guilty verdict. Silence loomed as the Judge read the jury's words.

"Regarding the count of first degree murder, we, the Jury, find the Defendant, Lauri Felder, guilty."

Shrieks and gasps rang in Lauri's ears as the shock assailed her. A part of her had prepared for a guilty verdict, but a larger part of her felt that the truth would prevail. She had just been rendered guilty of a crime that she had never committed while the real killer remained free with the ability to kill again. Lauri needed to cry or scream, even throw something, but her disbelief hardly allowed her to move. She stood, frozen and struggling to breathe, with her head bowed as panic set in, wanting to curse the jury for imprisoning a victim rather than find the murderer. She felt the hand of her attorney on her forearm.

"I'm so sorry," he apologized. "We will appeal this. It's not over yet. Stay strong."

"Ms. Felder, I hereby sentence you to the term of seventy-five years in prison, without the possibility of parole," Judge Holstein announced.

"Life," she repeated over and over in her head.

She would be incarcerated for the rest of her years, never to live normally again but to simply rot away in prison until she died. Lauri glanced to her left to find the Prosecutor smirking at her. The sight made her want to leap on the woman and attack her for destroying her life, but she thought better of it. Everyone had already dubbed her as violent and she didn't want to prove them right, even though she had nothing left to lose. The verdict devastated her.

"I'm innocent," she told herself. "I'm innocent." Suddenly, she found herself screaming it through the courtroom as two police officers handcuffed her. Being led out of court, Lauri blew a kiss to her bawling mother and sister, yelling, "I love you."

While her relatives consoled one another and Olivia DeFont celebrated another victory, Bruce sat with his head in his hands, knowing that he had helped to convict the woman he loved, and it was difficult living with himself at that moment. The guilty verdict divided the courtroom with some feeling like justice had been served.

Lauri was driven to a women's prison in a van with cages on the windows and doors, nearly one hundred miles away, where she was immediately forced into a small, concrete room with five other new inmates.

"You need to remove all of your clothing, jewelry, hair accessories and anything that may be hidden on or inside of your body," the female guard commanded. Lauri shamefully undressed, they way she had been forced to in jail when she was first arrested. "Turn and face the wall with your legs spread apart and your hands on the wall."

One by one, each inmate was felt up by another female guard with latex hands. Lauri was humiliated and uncomfortable at the awkwardness of being prodded by the stranger. The strip search finally ended and Lauri dressed herself in the gray prison suit that was issued to her before   being fingerprinted   and mentally evaluated by the staff psychologist.

"Do you have any tattoos or piercings?" He inquired.

"Only my ears," she answered.

"Are you taking any medications?"

"No."

"Have you been diagnosed with any mental or physical ailments?"

"No," she repeated.

The psychologist proceeded to ask if she ever heard voices, saw visions or felt as if she would hurt herself or others.

"I'm not crazy," she replied. She refused to admit that she'd been in the hospital for an attempted suicide.

"Clinically depressed?" He asked with raised eyebrows.

"No, my son was murdered," she explained.

"Do you have any thoughts at all about hurting yourself?"

"No," Lauri answered. She wasn't willing to allow the prison officials to lock her in a room by herself or put her in another hospital.

Given her crime and the circumstances surrounding it, the psychologist placed her on a twenty-four-hour suicide watch in a cell with cameras, near the officers' station, where she could be carefully monitored. The only thing that Lauri saw was gray steel and block. With its concrete walls and lack of sunlight, the cell block felt cold and depressing. There was no color, no life and, if she wasn't already depressed, she knew that her surroundings would certainly provoke it. Alone in the cell, she lay on the cot, sobbing uncontrollably while trying to wrap her head around her circumstances. This was her future, she thought. This was her new way of life, and learning to accept it was misery. She did think about ending her life and wished that her mother hadn't stopped her from it. There was no longer any reason for her to live, she felt. Her son was dead and prison was going to be her life. All she could do was cry and try to cope with it. She felt like she was suffocating and found herself nearly hyperventilating from the thought of it all. The camera revealed her struggle, and a guard entered quickly to assess her.

"I can't breathe," she tried to say but couldn't get it out. She couldn't catch her breath.

"It's okay," the female guard consoled, along with a nurse, who placed an oxygen mask over her nose and mouth. "Breath it in slowly and try to be calm." After a few minutes, Lauri felt her breathing normalize. "Do you usually suffer with asthma or other breathing problems?" Lauri shook her head. "Okay, just sit here with me for a few minutes and catch your breath," she said. Having the guard there with her seemed to help calm her while she took slow, deep breaths. "Are you feeling better?" Lauri nodded and took off the mask.

"I think I'm okay now," she told her. "It was just anxiety or something."

"This is why you're in this area for now, until you've come to terms with and adjusted to your surroundings," The guard said. "We can offer help when you're struggling." Lauri realized that she wasn't their first case and appreciated their care and urgency. She lie down and finally drifted off to sleep.

Her eyes later opened to an eerie silence with dimmed lighting, and she assumed it was the middle of the night. She lay on the lumpy cot with the blanket pulled up to her face as her reality settled back in. She realized that there was no way she could adapt to life in prison, and she developed a plan to get herself into general population, where she wasn't monitored as closely, and end her life. She drifted back to sleep and, the next morning, she was awaken by the sound of voices and the sound of the metal doors closing. She sat up on her cot and saw the guard station, where several of them busied themselves with paperwork. A few minutes later, the small, rectangular hatch opened in her door and a tray of food was set there for her. She walked over to take it and sat on the cot, nibbling on the buttered toast, but her stomach was repelling it. She knew that she needed to act as normal as possible to be transferred to general population so she forced herself to take bigger bites, even as sick as it made her feel. She choked down nearly everything on her tray.

"Well, look at that," a guard said. "You must have been hungry."

"Yeah," she fibbed with a dim smile, trying not to vomit it all back up.

After a full day of observation with Lauri appearing well enough for general population, she was transferred there.

The metal door buzzed as the guard led her in, lugging her bedding with her, and the other women inside the 2-story facility gawked suspiciously at her, some whispering amongst themselves about her. They stood on the balcony of the two-level facility while others sat at the metal tables scattered about. One wall held several pay phones, a water cooler and a microwave.

"You're home," the hardhearted guard commented and led her to a cell on the bottom floor. Lauri entered a tiny room of stainless steel and painted concrete floors where a dark-haired woman lay, reading, on the bottom bunk.

"Hi," she softly greeted her.

The woman peered up from her book, her suspicious eyes scanning her new, unwelcome roommate. Lauri took a deep breath and began unrolling the thin mattress on the top bunk. She felt the glaring eyes of her irritated cellmate following her every move, and it made her extremely uncomfortable. As she lay in her bed, Lauri wondered how she would survive her life sentence within those prison walls. She felt that there was no way of her making it through. Lauri couldn't live her life that way. She had hit an all-time low and truly had nothing left to live for. It felt to her like the walls were closing in. Panic consumed her as she envisioned her future as an inmate. Lauri knew that the only way out was death, and it was far more appealing than spending her life in prison. She wanted to be with her son. Her mind was reeling with methods of carrying out her wish.

"Just so you know, I'm not happy about you being here," she heard her new roommate say, "and we're going to have to go over the rules."

"Well, just so you know, I'm not happy to be here either," she replied.

"Chow," a guard yelled with an echoing tone.

She followed her cellmate to the tables, where a sandwich and soup were served on a cold metal tray. Quietly, she sat at a table among hundreds of strangers, all socializing as they ate, and although she had no appetite, she forced herself to nibble since it would be several hours before her next meal.

"What's your name, honey?" A spike-haired, stocky woman in her forties who sat across from her asked. She wasn't looking for friends but she couldn't afford any enemies either.

"Lauri," she replied softly to the woman.

"I'm Patty," the inmate said. "What are you in for?"

"Long story," she answered, not wanting to explain.

"Armed robbery for me," she informed Lauri. "I got fifteen years for holding up a bank teller at gunpoint."

It was the first time that Lauri had ever actually met a criminal, and she wasn't sure what to say or what reaction Patty was expecting, so she left it with a nod.

"How long you in for?" Patty inquired, and Lauri wondered if she was being nosy or just making conversation.

"Not long," was her response and Patty snickered.

"All the newbies say that," Patty replied with a snicker. "They all think their convictions will be overturned somehow. Don't fool yourself, honey. You're here for the long haul."

"That's what you think," Lauri thought, planning to check out as soon as she could.

Soon, the ten round, steel tables in the middle of the cell block were filled with socializing prisoners, some playing cards and dominoes, others braiding one another's hair and some just talking and laughing while they watched the single television that hung in one corner. She observed them closely, trying to decipher who was who. She watched them in their groups, engraving them in her mind to remember who was safe. Some, she discovered, were couples, holding hands and kissing as discreetly as they could without being caught. Lauri found a pay phone and called her mother.

"Lauri, honey, are you okay?" Her concerned mother asked, relieved to finally hear from her.

"Yeah, Mom, I'm okay. I guess I just need someone to talk to." Lauri wasn't okay. She was afraid and suffocating, but she couldn't bestow more worry on her mother.

"I promise to do everything possible to get you out of there. You don't belong there," her sobbing mother said.

"I know. My attorney is working on an appeal, so it will all work out." Lauri endeavored to keep a positive tone, never letting her mother in on her plan. As she spoke, a hand reached around and hung up the phone.

"It's my turn," the hateful voice of another inmate told Lauri and took control, shoving her away.

Stunned, Lauri turned to look her in the eye and saw the malicious grin of a dark-haired woman with tattooed arms. She walked away, obediently, when the woman began dialing the phone. Lauri didn't know what to do with herself. She felt like she would go crazy, confined in the concrete walls for the remainder of her life. In her bed she lay, staring at the concrete ceiling with her thoughts. She closed her eyes to induce sweet memories of Benny, the first time she held him after he was born, the way that his smile always evoked hers, his meek voice telling her he loved her. She held on to the way his arms felt around her neck and the aroma of his skin. Lauri missed Benny more than anything else in the world. Living without him was agony for her. Her sweet boy was gone and she was left to forever suffer without him.

The women's prison wasn't what Lauri had expected. Unlike a men's prison, the women, for the most part, appeared to get along and even support one another, except for one or two, who deemed themselves in charge of the others. They conducted themselves like the leaders of the pod. The women were gathered outside of their cells for most of the day and seemed to have more freedom than what Lauri had imagined, nothing like she had seen on television. It looked like prison but felt like a school or college dormitory, where everyone lived but moved about freely throughout the day. Even still, it was the last place that any of the women wanted to be. They were just trying to make the best of their situation. Lauri didn't care to be one of them. She didn't care to join in any of their groups or cliques and she didn't care to fit in. All she wanted was to be left alone in her own thoughts. She heard some of the more curious inmates whisper about her, and a couple even approached her, wanting to know her story. She wondered how they didn't already know, given its popularity in the media but, if they did, no one mentioned it. Lauri spent the entire day in her bunk, her mind reeling with reminders of her son and her life, when it was still good to her. She thought about Bruce and his betrayal. She wondered how her mother and sister were taking it all, realizing how difficult it must have been for them. It all made her feel horrible, and there was nothing she could do to fix it for any of them. She couldn't bear to live with the guilt of hurting them.

The days that followed were more of the same with Lauri, alone in her cell with her thoughts and three meals in between. Prison was already challenging her with its monotony and boredom, and being stuck with the same people everyday proved difficult. There were those whom she had dubbed the noisemakers, who were rowdy and energetic all day and night, endlessly yelling, laughing and running from cell to cell with no regard for anyone else. They annoyed her immensely. Then there were the couples who were always in the showers and bathrooms, leaving her only small windows of time to use them. There were the nosy ones who seemed to have made it their mission to find out all about her and then there were some, like her cellmate, who barely spoke at all. She hadn't spoken to her since they met and whenever there arose an opportunity to leave the cell, she did.

One afternoon, as she sat on her bed, three stone-faced inmates entered her cell, and it was clear that they were up to no good. Fear paralyzed her.

"Lauri, right?" One of them asked.

"Yes." Their visit made her suspicious.

"What do you have for us?" Another asked.

"What do you mean?" Lauri, inquired with baffled eyes.

"You better learn the rules, baby. You have to pay your way through here. You have to earn your place and your rights, and you need to know that there is a pecking order."

"I don't have anything," the terrified Lauri told them while acting unfazed.

"Nothing, huh?" One of the women said. "Well, you might want to find something because we'll be back tomorrow." The women left her cell with smirks on their faces and Lauri exhaled.

"What am I going to do?" She wondered. The trio obviously meant business, and she needed to acquire something for them. Lauri made her way to the pay phone to call her attorney. "I need you to put some money on my book by morning," she told him.

She requested eighty dollars as soon as possible, and he agreed.

As promised, the three women returned to Lauri's cell the following day.

"I don't have anything yet," she told them, "but he's putting some money on my book sometime today."

"It better be today because we need commissary," one responded with intimidation.

"She doesn't like running out of her shit," another commented.

"I told him as soon as possible." Lauri's heart raced, but she felt weak and humiliated for letting them intimidate her.

"You might want to call him back and tell him you need it now." All three exited her cell. To Laurie's relief, the money arrived later that morning.

"May I ask what you needed this for?" He inquired.

"It's to keep me safe in here and please, don't lecture me on it," she replied. "How is my appeal coming along?"

Ed assured her that he was working on it and would file it with the court as quickly as possible. Providing encouragement, he explained that even though the appeal process could sometimes take a while, he felt that there was a good chance of fighting her sentence.

"I hope so," Lauri said. "This place is killing me already. I just don't know how I'm going to survive this. I'm innocent. I don't belong here."

"I know, and I promise to do everything possible to overturn your conviction," Ed stated.

Lauri hung up with her attorney and located the bullies in the common area. They followed her to her cell, where she handed each of them twenty dollars and kept the remainder for herself.

"That's it?" One of the women replied. "Twenty dollars?"

"That's all that was left in my bank account," Lauri answered, hoping that they wouldn't see through her lie. The three of them stared at her suspiciously as if they were attempting to read her mind.

"This will get me what I need from the commissary for a couple days," the bully responded. "We'll be needing more after that."

"I told you, there's no more left." Lauri was shaken but firm. She feared for her safety but refused to keep paying for it. If it got around that she was paying them, she was sure that other inmates would soon expect the same.

"Well, honey, you'd better come up with something," another of the women said. "No one lives for free."

"Not peacefully anyway," another added.

With her head in her hands, she sat on her bunk, contemplating her next move. Her original plan of keeping to herself was only making her stand out more among the other inmates. She realized that she needed some allies. Lauri planned to begin with her cellmate.

That evening, she sat at the tables for dinner, scanning the prisoners, watching their demeanors and facial expressions, trying to decipher their personalities. No one else appeared to be a loner like Lauri. They all seemed to be part of one group or another, and she intended to fit into one for protection, though she feared that none would accept her.

Back in her cell that night, Lauri was surprised to see her cellmate staying in, and she approached her. She hadn't come off as the friendliest of people, but Lauri had to start somewhere. With a deep breath and an ounce of courage, she began.

"Michelle, right?" She peered up from her book, suspiciously.

"Yeah, why?"

"Prison life isn't easy to adjust to," Lauri said, nervously trying to strike up a conversation.

"Nope." Michelle hardly seemed to move beyond one-word answers, making Lauri's task even more difficult. She kept her eyes in her book.

"How long are you here for?" Once again, Michelle peered up from her book, this time with a sigh of annoyance.

"What difference does it make?"

"Okay, I get it," Lauri told her. "I was just trying to make conversation since we're living together now. I don't really know anybody yet."

"Yeah, well, it's the penitentiary, not high school," Michelle responded unenthusiastically.

"Yeah," Lauri mumbled, climbing up to her top bunk. She began writing a letter to her mother.

"Two more," she heard Michelle say, after a long silence.

"Huh?" Lauri spoke, unsure if Michelle was even talking to her.

"I have two more years in here," she said. "I've already done six." Her response took her by surprise.

"What for?"

"Why, you writing a book or something?" Michelle snipped.

"No, just making conversation again," Lauri snickered and sensed her cellmate's smile, too.

"You talk too much," her cellmate said. "It was prostitution and drugs. I'm not proud of it, but I was only nineteen years old and trying to make a living." Again, silence. "How about you?"

Lauri sighed with discomfort about displaying her life, but she couldn't ask another's business without discussing her own.

"I'm here for murder," she uttered softly, neglecting the details. Michelle looked stunned, expecting to hear Lauri say anything but that. She put down her book with intrigue.

"Get out! You don't look like you could hurt a fly. Let me guess, good life, bad marriage, husband either cheated on or beat you, or both."

"Yes." Lauri adopted that story instead of the real one. It kept her personal life her own. She had heard about people being killed in prison for child abuse, guilty or not. "I didn't do it," she added. "I was convicted of killing him, but I'm innocent."

"Honey, in here, we're all innocent," Michelle joked, "but if you're smart, you won't tell the wrong people in here that you're innocent. You're a new target with a girl next door face. You better find something to make you a little more intimidating."

"So I should just tell everyone that I'm a killer?"

"That's why you're in here, isn't it?" Michelle replied. "You should start with the three who keep taking your money."

"How did you know about that?" A surprised Lauri asked and Michelle snickered.

"I went through a couple hundred dollars when I got here. They do it to all of the newbies."

Lauri glared at her in amazement. Michelle was right. She needed to stand up to the bullies.

Chapter 9

Prison life hadn't eased up on Lauri since she'd gotten there. Everything was a learning experience and adjustment for her. She had, somehow, survived her first week of incarceration but it had been anything but easy. Everything there was so different than her life outside of the concrete walls. For her, the lack of privacy was the worst. She had always valued her privacy, but even using the bathroom was a public display in prison. With a metal toilet in a cell of two people, Lauri always waited until her cellmate was out for the undertaking. Showering didn't come any easier since there were no walls to separate the inmates. Lauri was always very conscious of the other women around her and, though most didn't appear to be bothered by the open concept, she yearned for privacy. It wasn't just the other inmates but also the female guards who were privy to the view of Lauri's nude body, and she was humiliated.

It was visitation day at the prison, and those who were expecting company had a spring in their step, anxious to reunite with their loved ones. To her surprise, Lauri was summoned to the visitor's area. She made her trek to a line of phones shielded by glass, only to find Bruce sitting there with the eyes of a puppy who was in trouble. Her heart fluttered as she questioned the intention of his visit. With a glare of hesitation, Lauri sat in the chair opposite him and picked up the phone receiver.

"Thanks for seeing me," he began with a face of sincerity. "I debated if I should even come here or not, and I drove a long way to see you, but I felt like I really needed to. Lauri, I came to apologize. It wasn't my intention for things to go this way. I was forced into a corner."

"Oh, you were forced into a corner? Well, what about me then? Look what I was forced into," Lauri coldly responded. "How could you do that to me? I trusted you."

"I know, and I wanted to tell you the truth because I discovered, early on, that you are innocent. I know you didn't do this."

"But you still helped put me in here," she replied.

"No, I was forced to testify. I testified to your innocence, and I'm still trying to prove that you didn't commit this crime. I meant what I said about falling for you, and you don't know what I went through having to do what they wanted."

"What *you* went through?" Lauri was appalled at his attempt to play the victim. "This isn't about you."

"I know that," he agreed. "It's eating me up that you're in here for a crime you didn't commit. I know you didn't commit it and I know how much you miss Benny. I asked them to remove me from your case but they wouldn't. I told them you were innocent, but they didn't believe me because they knew I had fallen for you." His guilty eyes fell to the floor. "I know I can't undo what's already happened, Lauri, but I can admit when I'm wrong and continue to try to help you. That's what I want to do." She let out a sigh. Part of her believed his words, and she felt foolish for it.

"You can't help me now," she replied icily. "Goodbye Sam, or is it Bruce?" She exited the area in anger, no longer interested in his explanation. He couldn't walk in her shoes to feel her agony. His life was still his own.

Lying in her bed, Lauri cried over what her life had been diminished to. She had only spent her first week in prison, and the mere thought of the rest of her life there ate at her. She felt that there was no surviving it. With her eyes closed, Lauri recalled the days when her life was serene and joyous, her days with Benny, laughing and playing, cuddling together with popcorn in front of the television. She could still hear his voice, almost as if he was right there with her, and she swore that she felt the warmth of his touch. Her heart ached for her son, and she couldn't understand why his life was cut so short. Benny came to her dreams, wearing the grin that he always carried when he sat on her lap, relishing her with his never forgotten embrace.

When morning came, Lauri was, again, beaten with reality. Benny was gone and her life was a convict's. She was barely off of her cot when the trio of women stood at her cell door, again demanding money.

"I don't have any," she insisted.

"You'd better get that fancy lawyer of yours on the phone again then," one of the women urged. Lauri was fed up. She refused to allow them to keep intimidating her. She stood, tall and courageous as her heart pulsated with fear.

"You're not getting another dollar from me," she barked with a face full of wrath.

"What did you say?" The youngest of the trio said, stepping toward Lauri.

"You heard what I said." Her fear had become fury and she had nothing to lose. "I'm in here for murder. I'm serving life so I've got nothing to lose. Go ahead and make my time worth it."

"Murder, huh?" The woman uttered. "Right. I doubt you have it in you."

"I'm here aren't I? Ask around." Lauri responded.

"You're such a joke, lady!" She quipped before the three of them disappeared.

Lauri sat on her bed, catching her breath as her heart palpitated out of control. She was proud of herself for standing up to them, but their intimidation and bullying infuriated her. She wanted her money back, even if it was only sixty dollars. It was about the principle. Standing up to the three women lent Lauri the courage to take back what they'd stolen from her, so she devised a plan to get her money back. She realized that the only way to get to the trio's money was to slip into their cells unnoticed during breakfast, when all three of them would be in the common area, along with most of the guards. Lauri hid in the shower area until all of the inmates were called to eat. Time was of the essence and it was important to be discreet. She darted into the first cell and began her search, checking under the bunks and pads but found nothing. She climbed to the top bunk to take a peek at some photos taped to the wall, which appeared to be the woman's children. Lauri noticed one photo in particular that stuck out and, when she carefully pulled it, she found a folded wad of money taped on the back. She taped the money to the bottom of her foot, with nowhere else to conceal it, and moved on to the next cell, which the remaining women of the three shared. Searching their photos and bunks revealed nothing, but she continued looking in every imaginable place while hoping that no one spotted her. With no places left to look, Lauri was convinced that the women had hidden their money elsewhere, outside of their cell. She glanced around for eyes before exiting their abode, and suddenly, "the sink!" She thought. Rushing back in, she pulled on the stopper and found it wrapped in money. With exhilaration, she hurried back to her hiding place before the other inmates returned.

Lauri couldn't believe she had even attempted her mission, but she felt such gratification to get revenge on the women who had demoralized her. She had gotten her sixty dollars back and left the rest of their money alone.

It didn't take long for the trio to find their money missing. Lauri watched them survey the cell block's inhabitants for answers. They had no idea who stole their stash and no one to blame it on. She was electrified over getting even. With the money in her hand, Lauri proudly pranced to the commissary with her grocery list.

A few days later, Lauri received mail, which she anxiously retired in her bunk to read. The first was a letter from Bruce.

Dear Lauri,

You have every reason to be angry for what I've done. I was wrong and I know that I hurt you, even though I didn't want to. Please believe me when I say that I didn't want to lie to you, but I honestly had no other choice. My job was at stake. I even tried to get out of the assignment and testifying but it was all to no avail. From the bottom of my heart, I apologize to you. I meant it when I said that I fell for you. I never meant to, but I quickly realized that you are everything I ever wanted in a woman. I fell in love with you. I desperately want to be in your life and I hope that you will allow it, even if it's only as your friend. Hope to hear back from you soon. I love you. Bruce

Even through the anger and betrayal, Lauri believed his words. She had fallen for him, too, and she did want him in her life, but she needed to know that she could trust him. On the other hand, how could she have a man in her life when she was incarcerated? She thought. It wasn't fair to expect him to stick by her. She continued to the other envelope, which was from her mother, and inside were photos of Benny. Lauri stared at them through her tear-soaked eyes. She missed him more than anything. The photos held the smile that was so precious to her. With a deep breath and wiping her drenched eyes, Lauri read her mother's letter.

Hello My Sweetheart,

I wasn't sure about sending these pictures, as I know they are bittersweet to see, but something inside of me felt that you needed them. I know that you are going through a lot there and it pains me, but I want you to know that I am doing all that I can to get you out. You don't deserve to be paying for something you didn't do. The people who know you know what a wonderful mother you are, and we know that you're innocent. Remember that I'm with you always, honey. I love you. Mom

Again, Lauri stared at the photos of her son,

wondering if he could see her from Heaven, if he could hear her when she spoke to him. Tears streamed down her cheeks as she yearned to hug and hold him.

"Is that your boy?" Michelle asked.

"Yeah," Lauri answered softly. "I miss him." Michelle handed her two photos.

"These are my daughters. I know what you're going through."

"No, you don't," Lauri thought to herself. Michelle had no idea what she was going through. She didn't know that her son was dead, and she didn't realize that Lauri was convicted of killing him. She didn't know that Lauri was an innocent woman in prison. They were nothing alike.

The approaching holidays seemed to lift the spirits of the inmates around her. Some had decorated the cell block with ornaments of paper and drawings. Lauri saw gleeful faces on her peers but she had no reason to celebrate. Christmas had always been her favorite time of the year, a time that both she and Benny loved. She'd had glorious memories of the holidays since her childhood, the aroma of the tree's fresh pine, the colorful décor and, most of all, the gathering of her loved ones. It was a tradition that Lauri had continued with Benny. Since he was gone, the holidays were merely one more reason to miss her child, her family, her life. In prison, all she had were memories of what once was. It was a time of grief and misery for her, and she just wanted to get the holidays over with as quickly as possible. Christmas would never again hold the same joyful meaning that it always had to her.

Weeks turned into months, and Lauri was beginning to accept that her life was behind bars. Her concerns had gone from paying her bills on time to what to buy from the Commissary and who she could trust around her. Prison was a different world with different issues. Lauri had accumulated a few more friends and had been receiving letters from Bruce and her family every week. He had even been back to visit her a couple of times. Lauri and Bruce had been slowly rebuilding their relationship. Though she couldn't understand him wanting to be with an incarcerated woman, she was grateful for his continued loyalty. Her mother was selling her house and moving into Lauri's to be closer to the prison. Guilt lived within her for her loved ones having to make all of the compromises that they were for her.

Lauri's attorney had filed the appeal in her case, and he was certain that her conviction would be overturned for lack of evidence. She had every hope in the world that she could go home, though she tried not to get her hopes up too high. With all of the ample time on her hands, Lauri had been skimming through law books in the prison library, trying to learn about the state laws for researching her case. Having a purpose helped her time in prison pass a little easier.

Lauri stood in the shower one morning, as she heard shouting coming toward her and growing louder.

"Child killer!" The voice yelled and, as she wiped the soap from her eyes, a young woman attacked her, knocking her to the ground and punching her in the head and face while screaming profanities at her and calling her names. Lauri felt each blow to her head, causing her ears to ring in pain. She felt her eyes swelling from the punches, and traces of blood blended in the water circled down the drain.

"Stop it!" Lauri screamed, struggling to fight the woman as her face was being held under the shower. She gasped for air as water poured down her throat, stealing her breath.

"You're going to die for what you did, bitch!" The inmate threatened. "You're a child killer!" With a handful of Lauri's hair, the woman rammed her head into the concrete shower walls as Lauri yelled for help. After what felt like an eternity to Lauri, two guards rushed in broke up the fight.

"Get dressed," one commanded as she helped her off of the floor.

Lauri was taken to the prison physician to have her injuries examined. Her nose was broken, she had a black eye and her head needed stitches. The pain was overwhelming, and she felt like she had just been struck by a semi. Both of the inmates were later ushered into a block room to present their versions of what had occurred.

"I was showering and she came out of nowhere, screaming and punching," Lauri told the group.

"Child killers deserve to be punched," the inmate rebutted. "I should've done worse to her."

Both women were sentenced to the segregation unit as punishment for fighting, where they would spend thirty days. Lauri lay on the cot, crying in pain and fear. She had never even seen her attacker prior to the fight, but the woman had discovered what her sentence was for, and Lauri swore that if the guards hadn't discovered them, the woman would have surely killed her. She worried that the other inmates would find out the truth, as well.

"How did I get here?" She pondered how her once joyful life had taken such a horrendous turn. Everything that could go wrong was, it seemed, as if her life was suddenly cursed. It felt like it had all happened in the blink of an eye. She would have given anything to turn back time.

Segregation, or the hole, as it was more commonly referred to, was lonely and barren. Each day in the cell, with little exercise and daylight, suffocated Lauri. She was permitted in a small, fenced area of the yard for one hour each day, where she savored the energy of the sun, walking circles around the perimeter or doing light exercise. As her wounds healed, she yearned to return to general population, hoping that no further threats came her way.

"Alright, you're going back," an officer finally informed her, and she was thrilled to be with people again. She was thankful to learn that the woman who had assaulted her had been moved to another area of the prison, but she hoped that word about her crime hadn't already gotten out to the others, realizing the dangers that went with it.

"Hey cellie, welcome back," Michelle greeted her. "It was getting kind of lonely in here without you. How was it?"

"Exactly what you imagine," she answered. "I'm so glad to be with people again."

A few weeks after she was released from segregation, Ed visited Lauri.

"What happened with the appeal?" She asked him, but his face already emitted the answer.

"Lauri, I am so sorry," he said. "The appeal was denied."

"What? No!" Her heart plummeted into her stomach as her hope faded away. "You said there wasn't enough evidence to keep me in here."

"That's true, but I just couldn't convince them," her attorney explained. "When a child is murdered and it's in the media like this, the state has to blame someone, anyone, because they can't look inefficient. In this case, they're blaming you, at least until they can find who's really responsible." It irked Lauri that Ed didn't appear more disappointed than he was over the verdict. His face didn't hint at any distress as he broke the news to her.

"Well, you have the money and your freedom, so I guess this is just another case for you, right?" She barked.

"I mean, this is my life, Ed."

"We can still continue appealing this, Lauri, even to the Supreme Court if we have to."

She sighed with her eyes to the floor. Her hopes had just been shattered. She was destined to live her life in prison, and she just couldn't understand why. What had she done to deserve it? The real killer remained free, and the thought of it was unbearable. Who had taken her son's life and why, she wondered. Lauri was afraid that more children would die. There was nothing she could do but cope with her circumstances. She sank into another wave of depression, existing only in her bed.

"Let's go," Michelle said sternly.

"I don't want to go anywhere," she whined. Her thin mattress and scratchy blanket that she once loathed suddenly provided her comfort.

"Come on, you're going," Michelle demanded. "You're just making yourself miserable and dragging me down with you." Against her will, Lauri dragged herself out of her bunk and walked with her cellmate to an unknown destination.

"Where are we going? I'm not in the mood for a counseling session."

"You'll see in a minute," Michelle rigidly replied. They walked into a large room of dogs, and the confusion was instantaneous. She wondered what the dogs had to do with her. The room that housed the animals was equipped with training tools, grooming tools, treats and dog toys.

"I should have stayed in bed," Lauri said before an attempted exit. Michelle grabbed her arm with force.

"Hey, I got you special permission to be here so have a little respect!" Lauri's eyes widened with alarm at her cellmate's tone. "These are seeing eye dogs, and I train them. Today, you're going to help me instead of moping around again." Lauri wasn't in the mood but she took Michelle seriously, and she had plenty of time to spare.

Michelle seemed to be a different person around the dogs. They appeared to soften her personality, and it was evident to Lauri how much they meant to her. She took her job very seriously, and the animals seemed to adore her.

"These guys make me happy," Michelle told her. "They really get me through the time here. You need something like this or you're not going to survive in here, Lauri."

The two worked with the dogs, training them to become the perfect aides for those who needed them and, before Lauri knew it, several hours had passed. Working with the dogs gave her time a purpose and, remembering Benny's love for animals, she felt him with her.

"So this is where you go all day?" Lauri asked her friend.

"Yep," Michelle confirmed. "Keeps me out of trouble and gives me something that is good for my soul. I never gave anything good to people when I was on the streets, so this is a great thing for me to do."

Lauri smiled at her with appreciation and she realized that outside of prison, she might have looked down in judgment at someone like Michelle, as if she were a drain on society, a drug-addicted prostitute with no ambition who chose the shady way of life. Michelle forced her to see that her presumption was far from the truth. Her new friend had substance and purpose, and it wasn't right to judge her for her life choices. Lauri realized that prison wasn't an institution of vicious criminals. Some had simply made bad decisions. She had a newfound respect for the women there.

"This place has a lot of programs like this one," Michelle informed her. Lauri was thrilled at the idea of having something to keep her occupied, and she appreciated Michelle for showing her a better way. She began looking at all of the prison programs, and art is what she chose.

It was a turning point for Lauri. She knew that she could either spend her time in prison, wasting away in anger, or she could choose to improve herself. It was time to stop blaming her circumstances and try to make the best of her situation.

In her research, Lauri also discovered a career program, which would allow her to work a daily job. She could cook in the mess hall or wash the linens in the laundry room. There were also opportunities to learn to be a travel consultant or hairstylist. She could select sewing or manufacturing. The options were plentiful as long as she maintained good behavior.

As a travel consultant, Lauri earned only cents a day at a computer, booking vacations by telephone, but it was enjoyable for her to view the glorious destinations. She stared at the picturesque mountains and beaches on her computer screen, imagining herself at each one and vowing that she would visit each if she was ever released from prison.

Three days of her week were occupied in the art program, where she painted the landscapes chiseled in her mind from her job. Her lack of natural artistic talent didn't matter because, for Lauri, her creations were therapeutic.

"I sold my house," her mother gleefully announced when Lauri called her, as she faithfully did each week. "Now, I can move into your house and be closer to you." She was grateful to have her mother closer to her, where she would be able to see her more frequently. Even though she couldn't be home, those that she loved were still there, supporting her.

Bruce faithfully continued his contact with Lauri through letters, phone calls and visitations. Every day, she was reminded of his loyalty and love for her, assured that he would remain by her side, even with her in prison. He hadn't missed a single visitation with her and, though Lauri always insisted that he deserved better, Bruce wouldn't hear of it. He was adamant about staying with her. It hadn't been easy learning to trust him again after all that had happened, but she found their relationship worth the work that it took.

Lauri's mother made a quick transition to her house, and she was thrilled to be closer to her daughter, where she could join Bruce for the visitations. Lauri was always elated to see them and talk to them, but watching her loved ones leave and return to the outside world was difficult. They carried away with them pieces of her heart. For them, it was equally as heartbreaking, being forced to leave her behind. Even still, they maintained the closest relationship possible.

With Lauri's new routine, prison life had become somewhat bearable. Occupying her time with positive things passed the days much faster for her. Aside from her job and her art classes, she dove into religion and studied law, making sure that she stayed busy so that her mind didn't have the opportunity to inundate itself with negativity.

Benny's birthday was quickly approaching, and Lauri dreaded it. She knew that it would be a day of sorrow but, in remembrance of him, she needed a special tribute. She searched her mind for the perfect idea, thinking about all of the things that she loved about him. Lauri decided that the best tribute was to see him again. She would paint him, a portrait of the sweet face that she missed so much.

On Benny's birthday, she rushed to her art session, anxious to begin her masterpiece and, though she was far from an artistic prodigy, the process, alone, she was certain would nourish her soul. With a blank white board in front of her and a paintbrush in her hand, Lauri closed her eyes to envision her son. Her strokes were flawless as she saw his soft and silky hair that she had combed every day, then his blue eyes, the windows to his soul, that had always mesmerized her. She saw his little button nose and the enlightening and contagious grin that melted her each time she saw it. Lauri mimicked every detail of her vision with soaked, proud eyes as she painted life back into her child. It was the most healing feeling in the world to her. When her masterpiece was complete, Lauri stepped back to examine her work.

"Oh wow! Just look at that," she said to her herself in awe. What she saw nearly stopped her heart. It was him, her son, and by giving him life again, she gave herself life again, too, and she felt renewed.

"Wow, Lauri, that's amazing," the art instructor remarked with vigor.

"Yeah," she tearfully responded with a proud smile.

"He must really inspire you," the instructor said as Lauri stared in amazement at his portrait.

"Always has been," Lauri softly replied.

Waking to see Benny's face in her cell every day brought fulfillment to Lauri. His memory had been perfectly captured in the painting of him, and it was her strength each day.

It was a visitation day and, as always, Lauri gleefully anticipated the arrival of her mother and Bruce. Their faces held distinctively secretive smiles.

"I have a surprise for you," Bruce told her as her elated mother looked on. Lauri's face lit up and, for a mere second, she thought that she was being freed from prison. He showed her a sparkling diamond ring. "This is to prove my love for you and to say that I'm here, supporting you. Will you give me the great honor of being your husband?"

Lauri stared at him, stunned. She was amazed that a man, especially a police detective, would choose a wife who was condemned to prison for life. In good conscience, she knew that it wasn't fair to him. Marrying him meant that he would be expected to spend his life alone, aside from the visitations and occasional conjugal visits. They couldn't even see one another without the glass window in between them. There was also his career that needed to be considered. He would be fired if the department discovered his relationship with her. Tears drifted down her cheeks.

"I love this so much," she smiled at him, "but I can't let you give up your whole life for me. I love you. I truly do, but this isn't fair to you. You deserve a normal wife and family, someone who can be with you in the right way. For that reason, Bruce, I can't marry you." Her empathetic eyes told a sad story of heartbreak.

"Lauri, I've already thought all of that through. I know exactly what my future would be. I realize that we would have a unique marriage. My life is complete with you, and I accept the terms because you're the one I love. You are my soulmate. I can't live without you, and this is what I want."

With flowing tears of joy and her heart overwhelmed with love, Lauri proudly accepted his proposal, amazed that someone could love her so much, especially in her situation. She wasn't permitted to hug and kiss him, or even hold his hand, so the couple was forced to seal their engagement by holding their hands against the glass. She couldn't even wear his ring.

In her bed that night, Lauri reflected on her previous couple of years. They had turned her life into a roller coaster of highs and lows but transformed her into a resilient woman with a positive outlook on her life. She was proud to have weathered such a monstrous storm and thought of herself as a survivor. She knew how proud Benny would have been in his mother.

Chapter 10

Because Lauri was a model inmate, the prison permitted the wedding, but Bruce was forced to exchange the diamond ring for a plain, gold wedding band, which was all that Lauri was permitted.

Two months later, her mother, sister, and Bruce arrived at the prison chapel. Lauri was an elated bundle of nerves as she prepared to give her life to her new husband. She put on the long, white sundress and makeup that her mother had brought her, and scooped her brown tresses back with the pearl barrette from her sister. For the first time in a couple of years, Lauri felt beautiful and she felt worthy. She looked to Heaven for her son's approval and said a prayer.

In front of her mother and sister, Lauri and Bruce were wed by the prison minister. The ceremony was short and simple but emotional as they tearfully exchanged vows, professing their undying love for each other. The guests were granted a quick reception, following the ceremony, where they celebrated with cake and toasted with paper cups of cider in lieu of champagne. It wasn't their ideal wedding day but, to them, it was still beautiful and filled with love. Bruce's parents and brothers had opted not to take part in the union, in disagreement of his decision to marry Lauri, but it didn't matter to him. He was marrying the woman he loved.

The newlyweds spent their first conjugal visit in a small, single-room cabin on the prison grounds. The undersized cabin had just enough space for a tiny kitchen and couch, petite bathroom and a bed. It was hardly as large as a hotel room, and the bare, block walls with a single window made it feel cold and barren, but it was all they had to call home for the weekend and they were happy to have it. Being Bruce's wife felt great to Lauri. His devotion amazed her, and they had a mutual respect for each other. She felt incredibly lucky to have him, and she was grateful.

Even still, neither Lauri nor Bruce was naïve of their future. Though they were married, they would spend their lives apart. Lauri hoped that he could handle their circumstances, but she worried that prison would eventually tear them apart.

"Are you happy?" She softly asked her new husband as they lay, him holding her in his comforting arms.

"Of course I am," he answered. "I'm the happiest man in the world."

"This won't be a normal marriage. This tiny room is basically our home together."

"I know, but I just married the woman of my dreams, and I wouldn't trade it for anything," Bruce assured her. "The rest is just stuff."

"You are such an incredible person, my husband," she said.

The two of them lay awake the entire night, talking, making love and relishing one another's company. Morning came all too soon, but they had the rest of the weekend together. Lauri was ecstatic to be able to cook her new husband breakfast and spend the day with him, even if it was in those less than desirable circumstances.

"I still can't believe you're here with me, but I'm so glad that you are," she told him.

"Me too," he agreed. "There's nowhere else in this whole world I'd rather be."

"Of all the things that have happened to me that I never dreamed would, marrying the undercover detective who helped put me in prison was definitely not one of them," she joked and they chuckled.

"Well, I guess some things are just meant to be," he ribbed.

"I wish Benny could have been a part of our wedding day," Lauri said.

"Me too, but I'm sure he was."

"Yeah," she said with a comforted smile. Bruce took

her hands in his and gazed into her eyes.

"I want you to know that I'm not going to give up on him, okay?" He told her. "I promise you, I'll keep looking for the person who did this and deserves to be here instead of you. I'm going to get you out of here." She desperately hoped he could deliver on his promise.

"I know that, babe," she replied with a smile. "Thank you."

"I love you so much," he professed.

"I love you, too," she replied with a kiss on his lips. "I wonder how I'll be treated in this joint now that I have a cop husband?" She ribbed.

The cabin was surrounded by barbed wire but, on its front porch were a pair of chairs and a swing. A small vegetable garden and several flowerbeds ornamented its small yard. Lauri and Bruce sat on the swing, soaking up the alluring sunshine, and Lauri relished it.

"I don't get the pleasure of this too often," she commented. "It's so nice."

"How is everything in here for you?" Bruce queried. "Are you doing okay?"

"Yeah, I really am," she answered. "I'll tell you, when I first got here, I really didn't think I would survive. I felt like my whole world was ending and I had nothing left to live for. It was horrible. I had decided, early on, that I was just going to end my life and get it over with because I couldn't face being in here every day, for the rest of my life. One day, Michelle picked me up out of my funk and forced me to see another way and, since then, everything has changed. It's like I saw daylight again, some hope for the future. I had to find something for myself that sort of gave me a goal, and I think the art classes did that. It took me a while but I realize, now, that I'm still living. It's just in a different kind of way. Prison isn't death. It's just a different world, and I had to find my place in it. Now that I have, I'm alright."

"You're such a strong woman. It amazes me, but I still worry about you in here," Bruce told her. "I feel so blessed to have you as my wife. I fell for you the minute I first saw you at the airport."

"I should have known that it wasn't just a coincidence meeting you there."

"No, it wasn't. The police department put me there to check up on you and befriend you, but I don't think they intended on it going quite this far," he joked. "I'm really glad it did though."

"Yeah, me too," Lauri replied.

The newlyweds spent their afternoon outside, talking and walking around in the yard, hand in hand. That evening, Bruce made his wife an Italian dinner with fresh salad from the garden before cuddling together on the couch to watch television.

"I could really get used to this," Bruce said, "even if it is right here in this small cabin."

"It is kind of romantic."

"We don't need anything but each other, sweetheart," Bruce insisted and Lauri felt the same.

Sunday morning arrived all too soon, and the couple dreaded having to part. Bruce promised to visit her the following week, and he left with a kiss. She was heartbroken to watch him go while she was returned to her harsh reality of the cold, prison walls. She would have given anything to go with him.

The day soon arrived for Michelle's release from prison and, though Lauri was enormously envious of her freedom, she was thrilled for her.

"You were my first friend here," Lauri told her. "You've taught me how to survive and made this life easier for me. What will I do without you here?" Michelle smiled.

"You'll be just fine, and you'll find a way out of here through those law books you're always reading." She paused with a sigh. "I'm really scared, you know? I've been in this place so long that I forgot how to live out there."

"You just stay tough, stay clean and keep your head up high," Lauri said, hugging her tightly. "You're a survivor, and you're going to do just fine."

"I'll miss you," Michelle sobbed.

"I'll miss you, too, but I don't ever want to see you come back here," Lauri told her.

A few hours later, her next cellmate, a newcomer named Amber, was ushered in. A young girl in her twenties with short, blond hair and innocence on her face, Lauri was reminded of herself as a new inmate. Amber appeared to be a frightened girl with a tough exterior who swore that she hadn't a care in the world, and it made Lauri want to save her.

"I'm Lauri. What are you in here for?"

"Armed robbery," she answered, casually, as if her crime meant nothing. "Me and a friend took a couple convenience stores. We were going to do a bank, too, until I was busted. Now I'm here for two and a half years."

The following day, Amber's tough persona showed itself with an irate inmate. What had begun as a disagreement between the two rapidly became a violent altercation of punching and kicking until Amber was stabbed by the inmate with a shank that she had made. Her wounds were minor, but both were punished by solitary confinement.

Three days later, Lauri returned to her cell to find a thin, long-haired woman in her 50s lying on her bed. She hinted of Indian descent and she was quiet.

"You must be my new cellie. I'm Lauri."

"Jonna," she greeted as she sat up. She peered at Lauri incredulously, investigating her face and demeanor without even a hint of a smile.

"Nice to meet ya, Joanna."

"Jonna, not Joanna," she clarified icily.

Getting a new cellmate was always difficult for

Lauri, being forced to live with a stranger who could be anything from a thief to a murderer. Their personality types were always a surprise, and all that she could ever do was hope for the best. Having no knowledge of her cellmate's crime was frightening but with Jonna's private demeanor, she thought it best not to pry.

The holidays were, once again, approaching as the inmates tried to make the best of them in prison. Many made paper decorations for their shared space and cells, and some created greeting cards for their loved ones outside of the prison walls. A group of four inmates created a Christmas tree from green construction paper, adorned with multi-colored paper ornaments, which they set on a table in one corner of the common area. The inmates worked joyfully together in the spirit of the holiday and, when they were finished, they admired their work, proud of what they had accomplished.

As always, Lauri thought of Benny, trying to guess which toys he would ask for if he was still alive. She imagined a glorious celebration in Heaven, which she knew that Benny was a part of. The memories of past Christmases with him crashed her mind, and she smiled at the visions of her son's surprised face as he opened each gift. If only she could have it all again but, in her mind, she relived their life together every day.

The abundance of holiday spirit in the pod elated even the hardest of criminals. The holidays offered new surroundings and a reason to come together in harmony, even if only for a short time. Nearly everyone seemed to put aside their differences and ill feelings for the cause. Even the prison guards seemed more friendly. The atmosphere held a more positive and gleeful aura, which invited even Jonna out of her private world. Lauri relished her surroundings, the vivid colors that brightly transformed the dull, gray steel, the warmth that Christmas always seemed to provide. For them, it was the next best thing to spending

Christmas with their families. That night, the guards on duty allowed them a radio in the Commons area, where the inmates danced and celebrated their Christmas together. Everyone appeared relaxed and happy, enjoying the fun that they had been missing for so long.

On Christmas Day, visitors flooded the facility, anxious to spend part of their holiday with the inmates they loved. Those who were considered outstanding prisoners were permitted visitations in a large, open room, full of round tables. Lauri sat with Bruce, Lana and her mother, talking and laughing for the four hours allotted. Lauri was thankful to spend Christmas with them any way that she could, and she appreciated them all giving up their day at home to spend it with her at the prison. Her only wish was that Benny could have been with them. The photo of him, placed at the empty stool at their table, was the closest that she could get. As they sat, Lana spoke of her work as a real estate agent and the events in her life. Her mother talked about her day to day activities and Bruce spoke of his investigative work. Lauri wished that she could speak excitement of something, but there wasn't much to discuss about prison. She described her paintings and her job as a travel consultant, and she talked about learning law and religion in her spare time. Her family was comforted hearing how Lauri's life had gotten better beyond the thick concrete walls. They worried about her there with all of the horror stories that they had always heard about prison. It was a relief for them to know that she had a different kind of life inside and that she was making the best out of her situation.

It saddened Lauri to watch her loved ones walk out the door when their visitation ended, but she felt lucky to have even had them there with her, knowing that many of the inmates had no one at all. Her wish was that, one day, she could walk out with them, but she knew that it could never happen. The rest of her life would be spent in prison, and there was no changing it.

That night, as she slept, Lauri felt a softness on her cheek and, as her eyes slowly opened, she discovered Jonna kissing her face.

"What are you doing?" She exclaimed as she sprung up in her cot, clutching her blanket. Her cellmate slowly backed away from her with eyes wandering Lauri's body.

"Don't you want to kiss me?" She spoke teasingly. "Let's have a little fun", she whispered with a devious grin.

"No, Jonna," she responded with an attempted politeness. "I, I'm not a lesbian."

"Well, not yet," she softly spoke, her hands caressing Lauri's face and neck and, as they began to lower, Lauri jumped down from her bed.

"No, Jonna, please, just stop," she pleaded, trying to remain calm, but her roommate persisted, backing her into a corner with her hands exploring Lauri's most private parts.

"Relax and have some fun with me," Jonna whispered, and Lauri was in a panic.

"Stop it, Jonna. I mean it!" She pushed her attacker's hands away and shoved her.

"Where are you going to go?" Jonna asked. "We're stuck in a locked cell together." She approached Lauri again, trying to pull off her clothes. Lauri continued to fight her off, threatening to scream if she didn't stop. When Jonna pushed her down on the concrete floor and lay on top of her, Lauri let out a shrill scream, triggering Jonna to leap off of her and onto her cot.

A male guard approached within minutes, peering into the small rectangle window of their cell door.

"Get to bed," he commanded in a deep tone and left.

Lauri climbed into her top bunk and bundled the thin blanket around her, tucking it snugly in on all sides of her. She shuddered in fear of another bout and refused to close her eyes. A few minutes later, she heard Jonna moaning from pleasuring herself, and it made her sick to her stomach. When Jonna finally grew silent and began snoring, Lauri drifted off to sleep.

"Thanks for nothing last night," Jonna told Lauri the next morning when the inmates were called for breakfast. Lauri drew her face to the woman's.

"I'm doing life for murder. If you ever try that again, I will cut your throat until you bleed out on this cold floor. You hear me?"

"You'd better hope I don't get horny again then," Jonna snickered as she walked out of the cell. Lauri's heart raced as she recalled what had happened the previous night. The thought of her cellmate attacking her again terrified her.

She spent the day as she always did, painting and working at her job and, when she returned to her cell just before dinner, Lauri found her painting of Benny broken up on the painted gray floor. The sight of it broke her and she wailed, picking up the pieces. It was obvious to her who had done it, and Lauri vowed to get her back. She called Bruce on the pay phone and told him what had happened with Jonna.

"You've got to let it go, babe," he urged. "She wants a reaction from you. Don't get yourself in trouble and ruin our visits together. Is she really worth that?" Lauri knew that her husband was right. As difficult as it was, she let it go and did her best to avoid her roommate for the next few days. Her next conjugal visit with Bruce was two weeks away and she didn't want to jeopardize her time with him. To her relief, Jonna left Lauri alone and had found a girlfriend to keep her occupied. Lauri did her best to stay out of their way and continue with her daily activities.

As the months passed, Lauri continued her activities in prison. Not only had she refined her artistic talent and accumulated a number of paintings, she was educating herself in law, as well, and was working on a degree. Lauri even filed another appeal, on her own, and was awaiting its review. She continued to work as a travel consultant, and Bruce and her mother still visited her whenever possible.

She had been in prison long enough that her life there felt almost normal. She had grown accustomed to it, almost comfortable even, and had forgotten what life on the outside was like. In her heart, Lauri was convinced that she was making the best life possible there.

Jonna had quickly become a hustler among the inmates, surviving incarceration the same way that she had survived on the streets. There was never a day that she didn't have the things that she wanted. Hustling was power for Jonna, and she had made a career of it. In addition to her relationship with Tasha, Jonna had several other girlfriends, all of whom she tutored in her game. She and Lauri hadn't had any other problems but still didn't make any effort to associate more than necessary.

Whether due to an anonymous tip or mere suspicion, several guards suddenly approached.

"Shakedown!" They shouted. Lauri and Jonna were immediately handcuffed and taken out of their cell so that it could be searched. Lauri wondered what it was that they were looking for as the guards ransacked their home, obviously on a mission. When they found nothing of interest to them, the cellmates were strip searched.

"What are you looking for?" Lauri curiously asked the guards. They proceeded on their mission, deliberately ignoring her question. The search yielded nothing and the duo was returned to their cell. "What was all of that for?" Lauri asked Jonna.

"Candy," she answered nonchalantly.

Lauri soon discovered just how naïve she truly was in prison when she figured out that candy was a code word for drugs. The guards had received a tip that Jonna was acquiring cocaine from one of her visitors.

"I'm not stupid enough to keep it in my cell." Though she didn't reveal the location of her stash, Lauri demanded that the drugs not be brought into their cell, and Jonna promised her that she wouldn't. Two weeks later, she was caught snorting cocaine in a closet and was sent to segregation.

Once again, Lauri found herself without a cellmate, but she appreciated the privacy, especially after all that Jonna had put her through. It wasn't easy sharing such close quarters, and a new cellmate meant starting over.

Lauri's next cellmate was a silver-haired woman in her sixties named Alice, who had just been convicted of murder for killing her husband of thirty-four years and his mistress. Alice didn't appear dangerous but merely scorned and, though Lauri couldn't condone her cellmate's crime, she understood. Her cellmate was hurt but vindicated. Like Lauri had once been, Alice was a loner, segregating herself from the rest of the population. She was down and depressed. Lauri recalled what it felt like, how long the days were, and her new goal was to find Alice a better life in prison. She wanted to give her cellmate the same gift that Michelle had given to her.

"Do you like art?" Lauri inquired of Alice.

"Yeah, it's okay, I guess," she answered with a dull tone.

"I paint a lot in here," she continued. "I thought maybe you'd like to go with me." When she appeared uninterested, Lauri added, "It will give you something to do."

"No thanks," Alice declined. Lauri took a deep breath, knowing that she should end the conversation, but she needed to rescue her new cellmate from the depths of her depression.

"I know how you feel," she told Alice. "I spent my first year here, just lying in that bunk, feeling like my life was over, but I'm in here for life so I had to find something to occupy my time." She knew that Alice had heard her words yet, still, she sat silent with disinterest. "Okay, well, I don't mean to push, but just know that there are programs here that can help make this place easier," and with that,

Lauri concluded the conversation.

Alice remained to herself, withdrawn and without words. She and Lauri spent the nights in their bunks, in silence, with Alice reading and Lauri penning letters to Bruce and her mother. All of her attempts to reach out to her cellmate had failed, and Lauri had annulled her quest of friendship, honoring Alice's wishes to be left alone.

On a visitation day, a few weeks later, Bruce arrived alone and informed Lauri that her mother was in bed with pneumonia and not fairing well. The news crippled her.

"She doesn't want to worry you, so she asked me to keep it quiet," he explained. Lauri was appalled that her mother would keep her illness from her. She worried about her, and Lauri's prison stay had only induced stress on her already fragile mother.

"Please, Bruce, promise me that you will take care of her, or call my sister, since I can't be there." He assured her that he was staying in the house with her mother until Lana would arrive, later in the week. Within two days, her mother's condition worsened and she was hospitalized. Lauri was dying inside, knowing that she couldn't be there with her. She couldn't even call her and it tore her up inside. Her mother had always been there for her but she couldn't do the same. All that she could do was continue writing her letters and cards every day.

Lana arrived with Bruce at the next visitation.

"Mom is getting worse," she informed her sister. "It's a struggle for her just to breathe. The doctors say she has fluid in her lungs."

Lauri bowed her head with the tragic realization that her mother was living her last days. She had to prepare for another devastating loss and the mere thought was unbearable. The heartbreak overwhelmed her as she sat, without words, with her sister's pain glaring at her.

"I can't even go and see her," Lauri finally spoke, tears stinging her eyes as she shook her head with disappointment.

"She understands, sis, and she knows that you love her," Lana consoled.

One week had passed when Lauri was informed that her mother had died. The past came back around as, once again, she lie in her bunk, mourning the loss of someone that she loved. A lifetime of memories played in her mind, flashing visions of her mother's smile. She remembered her hugs, and her voice, her elegant aura, her positive words of wisdom and encouragement. Lauri's mother had always been a representation of strength and beauty, someone whom she felt was a great contribution to the world, and she would be profoundly missed. It tormented Lauri that she wasn't permitted to spend her mother's last days with her.

Because she was a model inmate, Lauri was granted special permission to attend her mother's funeral, though she had to be escorted by a police officer. She was grateful for the opportunity to say goodbye to the woman who had so graciously influenced her life. She looked at her mother in the silver casket, her frame small and frail and her cheeks sunken in, and it was almost like seeing a stranger. The woman in the casket didn't look like her mother. Her body had deteriorated rapidly during her illness. Guilt ravaged Lauri as she stared at her mother's lifeless shell and she cried for her.

"I'm so sorry, Mama. I'm so sorry that I didn't make your life any easier. I know you're with my Benny now, smiling and dancing." Part of her wished she was there with them.

"Are you okay, honey?" Bruce consoled with his arm around her.

"Yeah, I will be," she responded, but she knew it would take a long time. Her mother had always been so important to her. Losing both her son and her brought Lauri to her breaking point.

"Mom really suffered at the end," Lana told her

sister. "Now, she's free." They held each other, crying for the woman who had raised them.

Lauri felt that she owed her mother a tribute and, as with Benny, she painted her portrait and brought back her beauty and elegance. When it was complete, she followed it up with a masterpiece of her mother and son together, to compliment her expanding art collection.

Alice approached Lauri, one evening, in their cell.

"Your paintings," she began, "do they help you get through your days here?"

"Oh, definitely," she responded. "You wouldn't believe all that art has gotten me through. It's very therapeutic for me. I was never even into it before I came I here." Her cellmate nodded her head, in thought, while Lauri explained to her the variety of programs that the prison offered. "My first cellie, Michelle, trained seeing eye dogs when she was still here."

"I never worked the whole time I was married, but I always wanted to be a beautician," Alice said. In the prison, she could learn the trade. The thought of it seemed to lend Alice hope and give her something to look forward to. It was the first time that Lauri had seen a spark in her cellmate.

That night, the two women sat in their abode, talking for hours. Alice spoke of a subservient life with her husband, how she had neglected her own dreams and passions to support his. She had devoted her entire life to him, even through his many affairs. She had found satisfaction in being a housewife and mother, and her family was her world.

"My whole life, everything I knew, was shattered with his last affair because he wanted to end our marriage for her," Alice confessed. "The others were flings but he actually fell in love with the last one. I just couldn't take it. It destroyed me, the pain and humiliation, all that I had given up for him. It was like none of it mattered. He just wanted to replace me with her. How could he be willing to throw away all of those years and memories so easily for someone he barely even knew? I had made him my whole life. I mean, I did everything for him, catered to him and his family." Lauri's heart ached for Alice as she listened to her words. "What I did to them was wrong, I know but, at that time, I just felt that they deserved it." She had killed for both love and hate, destroying their lives like she felt they had destroyed hers. Still, her vindication had only frozen her hardened heart, and she expressed to Lauri her need to recover the warmth and passion that it once held.

Alice appeared genuine, and Lauri found a sense of trust in her. She opened up to her about what had happened to Benny and how she was falsely convicted of his murder.

"You are the only person in here that I've told that to," Lauri said. "I just don't want people to think that's who I am, a child killer, because I'm far from it." She and Alice formed an unbreakable bond that night, a friendship built on trust, and they vowed to take care of each other in prison. In those walls, they were sisters.

Lauri's continued studies soon paid off when she earned her master's degree through the mail. Her accomplishment thrilled her, and she was more proud of herself than she had ever been before. If only her knowledge could free her, she thought, as she continued toward a law degree. She had lived eight long years in prison, and it was almost difficult to remember a life of freedom. The institution had become her home.

"I'm so proud of you, babe," Bruce told her. "No one deserves this more than you, and I always knew that you could do it. Once you finally earn that law degree, you'll be unstoppable!"

Lauri had thrown all of her free time into painting and studying, and both had paid off in many ways while also making her time in prison bearable. Her life was completely different than on the outside but, in many ways, therapeutic and beneficial. She knew that she would never have had the time to pursue either of them outside of prison, but Benny was her muse. She garnered the will from him, and she knew that he would have been proud of her.

Prison was a world of its own with most of the same people, day in and day out. Some were easy to bond with while others passed their misery onto whomever they could. Most of the women in Lauri's pod had become like family to her through the years and, somehow, she had simply adjusted to spending her days there. She invested her time in being busy, helping others, involving herself in therapy groups, her job as a travel agent, her studies, whatever she could to pass the time more quickly but, even so, she never lost sight of her top goal, which was finding Benny's killer and her freedom. Every year on his birthday, Lauri did a special painting and birthday card for him in celebration. He would have been a teenager by then, she thought, as she tried to picture what he would look like.

"I just know that he would be so handsome," she told herself. He was always in her mind and heart, always a part of her that she would never forget but, even all of those years later, there still hadn't been a break in the case. No other evidence or suspects had come to light, and it seemed that the case had simply grown cold. Several times, she had even written to the courts and police departments to have the case turned over to a fresh set of eyes, but it was no avail. They already had their suspect, as far as they were concerned. All of her appeals had been exhausted, so she was left to simply do her time and hope for a miracle, at least until she earned her law degree and could help herself.

Following her mother's death, Bruce moved into Lauri's home and continued to visit her every week, faithfully. He was completely committed to her and worked tirelessly writing letters to the parole board for her release. She and Bruce were permitted conjugal visits every other month, and they always looked forward to their romantic weekends in the tiny prison cabin, pretending that they were somewhere else while enjoying one another's company. They loved being able to cook meals together and snuggle under the blankets, holding each other for hours. The couple made the best of every minute they were allowed together. He was what kept her going.

Lauri worked endlessly on her law degree, constantly reading, studying and writing essays. She was convinced that it was one of the most difficult challenges of her life, but her determination wouldn't allow her to quit and, five and a half years later, she finally earned her degree.

"You are such an inspiration to all of us," Alice told her. "I'm so very proud of you, girl."

"Now you can help all of us out with our cases," another inmate said.

Lauri felt like she had shed blood, sweat and many tears to earn it, and she was proud of herself. She had come such a long way from where she began.

With her law degree, Lauri began writing letters to court Judges, attorneys and local government officials regarding her case, requesting that all of the information and evidence be reviewed again. The letters detailed how she was accused due to lack of evidence. For fifteen years, a murderer had been free, and she wanted the justice that had been stolen from her. She wanted the real killer to pay for his horrific crime.

Two weeks later, a young, dark-haired man, who looked to be in his early twenties, came to see Lauri as a result of one of her letters. He introduced himself as Michael Foley, an intern with one of the law firms who had received her letter.

"Your story is fascinating, and I think that it will challenge me as an intern." He told her. "With your permission, I would like to work with you on it."

Lauri glared at his youth. She had hoped for the attention of someone with more expertise, but she would accept all of the assistance that she could get, so she agreed.

"You're probably around my son's age," Lauri told Michael with a smile and, when he smiled back, she found comfort in him. His honest eyes invited her trust, empathizing with her thoughts and suffering the anguish that she still felt from losing Benny. The young man's strong facial features reminded her of someone she knew but couldn't quite pinpoint. Michael spoke with compassion and humanity, as if he understood her circumstances, and he appeared genuine to her cause.

"I would like to get your file and a copy of the court transcripts to look through, if that's okay with you," he said. "I will also obtain the police report and records to evaluate their investigation."

"That would be great," she replied with appreciation. Lauri was comfortable putting her faith in her new ally. Though his age and inexperience left her uncertain, she could see that he was eager to make a name for himself, and she felt that it could also work in her favor. There was something about the young man that Lauri trusted.

Of all the letters that Lauri had sent, only two other responses came, both of them refusals to reopen her case. She needed to have the lack of evidence reevaluated, and she had to force the court to see that someone was getting away with murder. In the court's eyes, the killer was behind bars and the case was closed. She knew that it would take something profound to make them revisit the eighteen year old case.

Lauri was granted another conjugal visit with Bruce that weekend. She was elated to spend some alone time with her husband. In the small cabin, she was a wife to him, cooking dinner on the small stove, massaging his shoulders and holding him in her arms. She had the opportunity to cater to him, the way that he always catered to her. Lauri wanted to show her appreciation for him and his loyalty. Bruce had been by her side, just as he'd promised her, for fifteen years and, even as husband and wife, they lived their lives alone, forced to spend their lonely nights apart. Even after so many years, they had never grown accustomed to their situation but hoped for the day that Lauri would finally be home. Prison was a challenging place to maintain a marriage but, somehow, she and Bruce had weathered the storm and made it work. He had spent his years loving her through daily telephone calls and sporadic visits to the facility but it always seemed enough for him. Even when Lauri had offered to free him of his lifestyle through divorce, Bruce refused, assuring her of his unwavering love. Making love to him lit fires of ecstasy within her, and she felt as though she couldn't get enough of him. As they lay, entwined, they professed their love and devotion for each other. She made sure to relish every sweetened minute in her husband's embrace. Their time together was more precious than anything else in the world to them and they treasured it.

"I wish we could do this every night," Bruce lovingly told whispered. "I miss you so much when we're not together."

"I would give anything for that," she responded with a smile but still frustrated by the thought of living their life apart. All that they had was a weekend together every other month but always, they made the best of their time together.

The dreaded morning arrived and Lauri savored their final moments alone together before, again, they parted. Leaving her husband was never easy and, each time that they were forced to say goodbye, Lauri couldn't help but fear it being their last.

Chapter 11

A couple of weeks passed before the fervent law intern made his way back to see Lauri. He had studied her case intensely for new information that he could use to help prove her innocence.

"I saw some discrepancies in the documents that I think could be used to show incompetency of the prosecution to prove guilt," he mentioned. "There is a real lack of evidence in this case, not to mention a pretty defective police investigation. It's almost as if they hurried through it to blame someone, perhaps to satisfy the public, given all of the media attention that the case generated." Lauri had to admit how impressed she was with his intellect. His young age and inexperience hadn't lent her much confidence in him initially.

"My attorney filed appeals based on that, but they've all been exhausted," she replied.

"Yes, I definitely see that, but I found a few things that weren't mentioned in his appeals."

"Well, anything is worth a try at this point," Lauri said. "I've been in here way too long."

"Yes, you have because I believe you're innocent," he told her. She relished his confidence. "On a personal note, the house address really caught my attention because I actually lived in that neighborhood for a little while, as a kid," Michael told her.

"Really? Wow, what a small world," the amused inmate replied. "You might have known Benny. Which house did you live in?"

"Well, I'm not sure because I was so young but I do recall the street name," he said.

"Amazing!" Lauri exclaimed. She asked about his parents, wondering if she knew them. Michael explained to her that his father had raised him.

"My mother died when I was five years old." Lauri

was amazed at all that they had in common, and it strengthened her trust in him. She wondered how they had never crossed paths before then. "Since my father was out at sea with the Navy, I stayed with my aunt, out of state, for a few years after her death. My father just recently passed away."

"Oh wow, I'm so sorry," she replied sympathetically.

"Thanks. Garrett Foley was a great man," Michael spoke respectfully of his father. Lauri peered at him suspiciously, feeling like she was trapped in the twilight zone. Benny's father's middle name was Garrett and he, too, had recently died.

"It can't possibly be the same person," Lauri told herself. Her ex-husband's last name wasn't Foley and he had spent years in prison, not the military. Still, Garrett wasn't exactly a common name, which she found to be a striking coincidence.

"Getting back to your case, I've reviewed all of the information," Michael told her. "I have to agree with you that there are a lot of holes in the investigation, most of all the serious lack of evidence. I got the law firm involved, and we are going to help you."

"I can't pay for your services," she reminded him.

"The firm has decided to help you pro bono, so you won't have to pay if we don't win your case," he explained.

Lauri was grateful for any help that she could get and, though she had no idea what their plan of action was, she put her faith in them, hoping for the best.

Bruce visited the next day, and Lauri told him what Michael had said. Her voice hinted of rejuvenation as she spoke, concerning Bruce that she was getting her hopes up only to be let down again.

"I'm not naïve to the situation, but there's just something about Michael that I believe in. It's a gut feeling," Lauri proclaimed. She felt a friendly connection to him, as if she had known the young intern for years. Whatever it was about him, her instinct led her to trust him. "Besides, he's my last hope of ever getting out of here."

In the several days that followed, Michael frequently invaded her mind, not because of his empathy for her but because of her empathy for him. His sad story of losing his mother as such a young age stuck with her, and she had compassion for him. Lauri was missing her son and Michael was missing his mother, and she felt that it somehow brought them together because they could sympathize with the other's grief. They lived in parallel worlds, it seemed, which made understanding one another easy.

During his next visit, a couple weeks later, Lauri felt compelled to express her sympathy.

"Before we start, Michael, I just want to say, again, that I'm really sorry about your mother. It has really stuck with me. With losing my son, I know how it feels."

"Thank you. I appreciate that," he said. "I wish I could remember a little more about her."

"May I ask what her name was?"

"Laura Foley," he replied with a sad smile as he proudly spoke her name.

"Forgive me for all of the questions," she said. "It's just uncanny how many coincidences there are between your life and mine."

"I have to admit that it's pretty crazy," he responded. "Did you know my parents?" Having lived on the same street, she was surprised that she didn't.

"No, it's just..." Lauri thought twice about reopening old wounds. "Nevermind, it's not important."

"What is it?"

"Well, it's probably nothing but my ex- husband's name was Kevin Garrett Felder, which is just really close to your father's name, Garrett Foley, and he just recently passed away also," she said. "Your mother's name was

Laura Grossman-Foley and mine is Lauri Felder, which are also really close to each other." It was something she just couldn't ignore. Her heart skipped a beat. She sat, frozen and stunned, with his words ringing in her ears, wondering if she could possibly be looking at her son. "No, it can't be," she thought. There had to be another Laura Grossman. The police had confirmed Benny's death. Still, there were overwhelming consequences that she couldn't ignore. Benny's father's name was Kevin Garrett Felder, a name very similar to Michael's father's. It played over and over in Lauri's head. In disbelief, she struggled to speak.

"Michael, my birth name is Laura Grossman." He stared at her, stunned at the revelation. Neither he nor Lauri could rationalize it, but the coincidences were enough to provide both of them with a lot of questions. "My husband's middle name was Garrett. You lost your mother at five, the same age that my son was when I lost him."

"I can't believe this," he said, noticing her features in him. They sat, staring intently at each other, both wanting to believe that they were mother and son, while at the same time fearful of the truth. The two of them compared names, craving answers. "My father was in the Navy, but didn't you say that Benny's father was in prison?"

"That's right," Lauri replied, "but he was in the Navy before that." She was on a quest for the truth, and they needed a way to find it. Just then, it hit her. "Do you have a birthmark under your left arm?" Michael grew pale with shock as he nodded his head to confirm it. "Oh my God, Benny!" Lauri erupted into tears and flew out of her chair to hug him. He held her so tightly that it took their breath away. "Oh my God, I can't believe it!" She echoed. "It's really you." Together, they cried in an embrace that neither was willing to break.

"I can't believe this," he sobbed. "I'm hugging my mother." When they finally separated, they sat closely, holding hands and talking about their lives, trying to figure out how they had been ripped apart for so many years.

"I looked for you for so long, and then the police told me you were found murdered," Lauri told him. "They said that your dental records matched that little boy." Her disbelief slowly became anger. "I don't understand this."

"I don't remember being taken from you, but I lived with a woman named Jean, whom I was told was my aunt, until my father came back." Lauri searched her past for a woman with that name but came up with no one.

"So, your father moved you out of state and had you all of those years, and then he told you that I was dead so that you would never look for me," Lauri said, her intensified ire attempting to overtake her. "He must have changed your name, too, because it was Benjamin Lee Felder,"

Benny went on to explain to Lauri how he had been home-schooled and kept somewhat isolated from other people. He had always wondered why their life was so private and in talking with Lauri, the pieces were coming together. They were both dumbfounded as to how Garrett had pulled off such an elaborate scheme for so long. Lauri had endured years of torture because of him, and she swore that if he wasn't already dead, she would kill him herself for it. Having her son back after so many years was a miracle that changed her life within minutes.

Lauri told him about her paintings of him, and she was anxious to show him the photos of him as a child. They had been robbed of their time together, time that they could never get back. There was so much to talk about, so much that she wanted to say to her son.

"I'm going to get you out of here, Mom," he told her, and his words thrilled her. "You've been through enough."

"You called me Mom," she replied with a tearful grin. It had been years since she had been called that, and it was a word that she thought she would never hear again.

In just two hours, Lauri's whole life had changed, and she couldn't wait to give Bruce the news. Having Benny back was surreal, and she prayed that it wasn't all just a dream. She ran to the phone to call her husband, and when she told him, he was flabbergasted.

"Are you sure it's really him?" He asked, concerned that her desperation for her son was duping her.

"I'm positive. He's been alive all these years, living privately with his father," she said as she relayed Benny's story to him. Bruce was full of questions but thrilled over the news. He would be getting his wife back, and he had a stepson.

"We're getting you out of there, baby," he gleefully chirped. "I always knew there would come a day when the truth would finally come out."

The law firm immediately filed a motion for Lauri's release when the attorney heard the story. Benny underwent the DNA testing that was required to prove him as her son.

"I pray so much that I'm him," he told her. She was wrought with nerves while they waited for the results.

"This is the most incredible story I've ever heard!" Alice exclaimed. "I really hope it's him."

They would be filing charges against the police department who convicted Lauri, but their first priority was to have her immediately exonerated of all charges. Within just days, Benny returned to the prison to free his mother and take her home.

"The test came back," he said. "I'm your Benny." Lauri couldn't believe her ears. It was the miracle she had always wished for.

"Lauri, I'm so happy for you, but I'm really going to miss you," Alice said as she hugged her.

"You stay strong," Lauri told her with a smile of tears.

"Are you ready?" Benny asked.

"Oh yes, I am so ready," she answered, and with that, she headed for freedom. Outside of the prison walls, the sunlight was gold on her face. Relishing the moment, she took a deep breath and smiled. Her dream had come true. Lauri turned to bid farewell to prison, but the hard lessons it taught her would forever remain.

With news of her release, a media frenzy stood outside of the prison gates, awaiting a comment from Lauri.

"How does it feel to be a free woman?" One reporter yelled as she and her son slowly drove off. She looked at her son and smiled.

"It feels great," she told him.

At home, a celebration of balloons and friends awaited her. Lauri ran to Bruce, squeezing him tightly. "Welcome home, baby," he greeted her.

"It's so great to be home," she replied with a grin. The familiar smell of her home welcomed her as she walked through each room, soaking up the memories. "Benny, come and see your room," she told him and led the way. The room was exactly how she had left it, even after all that time. He walked in, looking around as if trying to recognize anything that he could. "This is where you were taken from, and I slept endless nights in your bed, just praying for your return." She sighed, fighting back tears. "This room used to hold so much sadness for me, and now..." her words were cut off by sobs as she broke down. Benny held his mother as she cried. "It's all over now, Mom," he consoled her. She had almost ended her life to try and be with him, but that moment made her so thankful that she had been stopped from it.

The celebration continued with the media surrounding her house, still attempting their story.

"They've been with me through all of this," Lauri said. "I'm finally going to give them their story." She led Benny outside to them. "This is my Benny," she said. "He's alive, and I've been exonerated. Please, we need our privacy now." With that said, they walked back into the house.

After the party, Lauri sat with Benny and Bruce, talking about the events of all those years ago. They told her son about how Bruce was there through all of her pain with Benny's disappearance and assumed murder. She explained to him all that she endured, searching for him and living through his absence, and as Benny listened to their words, he shook his head, apologetic for her grief.

"I wish I'd have known," he said. "All of those years, I thought you were dead, and life was so hard growing up without a mother, especially not being able to remember you. My father didn't even have a picture of you. He told me that you loved me, but that you had died in a car accident."

"This is such a miracle," Bruce said. "Now, we can finally be a family."

That night, Lauri and Bruce cuddled in their own bed, and she relished how good it felt to be home. Her nightmare was over, and she finally had her life back.

The days that followed were bliss for Lauri, and she savored every minute. Every room of her aged house emitted sweet memories of the years long gone, and it was a strange feeling, leaving her home with Benny a child, and returning with him an adult. She had lost so much of her life that she could never get back, and it didn't seem fair. Still, she had her son back, and that was worth her years in prison. Lauri felt like she should be out, enjoying her freedom, but leaving her house was a struggle. For so long, she had kept the same schedule and had her activities dictated. Walking out, into freedom, terrified her. Suddenly, the world seemed enormous and frightening. She was accustomed to boundaries, and having none made her nervous.

She soon found herself in yet another battle. Lauri needed to find out the real identity of the boy whom she was assured was Benny, eighteen years before, and she needed to know who the man was that kidnapped him. Lauri and her son sat in the law office, where he was an intern, talking to the attorney.

"Okay, so let's try and figure this out," the attorney said. "A man stole you from the home when you were five years old and took you to a woman named Jean, whom you were told was your aunt."

"Yes, but it turns out that I never had an aunt Jean, so I don't know who she was," Benny replied. "I wasn't even with her long enough to know her last name."

"Then your father came, several weeks later, and moved you to another state, telling you that your mother had died in a car accident?"

"Yes."

"Lauri, did the police ever question him after Benny's disappearance?" The attorney asked. She explained that the investigators had spoken to him in prison and quickly eliminated him as a suspect. She was already in prison when he was released, and the case was already closed.

"The police told you that they had found a murdered boy whom they believed to be Benny, and they later confirmed it with dental records."

"That's right, so who is that little boy?" Lauri wondered.

"I'm going to file a request for the body to be exhumed and tested. In the meantime, we should gather the necessary documents – birth certificates, social security cards, even school records for Benny. Your father obviously had your name changed, and we need to track how and when he did it. It would be extremely beneficial if we could find this woman, Jean, but that might not be possible."

"I wish my father was still alive to answer some of these questions, since he was obviously behind all of this,"

Benny responded in anger.

The motion was soon approved, and two weeks later, the boy's body was exhumed for testing, but after so many years since his death, it was nearly impossible to identify him.

"For so long, I thought that little boy was you," Lauri told her son. "Maybe this will give his mother some peace."

It took weeks for the test results to come back, and finally, the boy had a name – Michael.

"His name is Michael Foley," the attorney informed Lauri and her son. Benny grew pale.

"That was my name," he said in a stunned tone.

"I know, and this opens up a lot of doors for us," the attorney remarked. "I began searching and found out that his mother's name is Eugena Foley."

"Jean," Benny replied, shocked at the discovery. His identity had been switched with the expired child's, and, moreover, Jean was his mother. "What is going on?"

Lauri sat, dumbfounded, desperate for answers. It was as if her ears were playing tricks on her, and she was lost in confusion.

"I'm going to take this information to the police and have them locate her," the attorney told them.

The police were able to locate Jean a few weeks later, and they brought her into the station. After several hours of questioning, she finally broke her silence.

"I had a relationship with Garrett," she spoke of Benny's father. "I loved him." She dropped her head and sobbed. "I was a prostitute when my son was killed by one of my clients. Garrett felt responsible because he managed me from prison."

"He was your pimp?"

"Yes, I sent him money in prison, and we were going to get married when he got out. The client was his friend." Jean wiped her tears with a sniffle. "He paid one of his buddies who had just been released from prison, to get Benny for me as a replacement for Michael, my son," With a sigh of frustration, she continued. "I really thought he loved me, but when he got out of prison, he took Benny and left me."

"Why didn't you go to the police?" The officer asked.

"I saw the search for Benny on the news and I thought about calling, but I was already an accomplice to the crime." After another sniffle, she confessed, "I wish now that I had." With the detective's urging, Jean revealed to him the kidnapper's name.

"What about the dental records?"

"Detective Nelson was my best customer," she answered reluctantly. "He needed a suspect and I needed a son. We switched the dental records."

The attorney relayed Jean's information to Lauri and Benny as they sat, in disbelief, absorbing his words. "This was a pretty elaborate scheme."

Suddenly, it made sense to her why Detective Nelson had been so quick to accuse and convict Lauri of the crime. He had been involved the entire time. Bruce had no knowledge of their scheme and had merely been used as a pawn in the bogus investigation. Jean, the two detectives in the case, and the kidnapper were all arrested immediately and jailed while the attorney built his case against them. In court, the following year, their sentences were handed out. Jean was sentenced to seventeen years in prison, and her accomplice was sent back for fourteen years on the kidnapping charge. Detective Nelson, who had already retired, was sentenced to nine years for his role, and since his partner had confessed in jail and testified against him, he received a lesser sentence of five years in prison.

Once and for all, the nightmare had ended for Lauri, and she and Benny were ready to put it all behind them. Together, their lives could begin again.

www.ingramcontent.com/pod-product-compliance
Lightning Source LLC
Chambersburg PA
CBHW051831170626
46807CB00003B/1128